Hope

Stories from a

Women's Refuge

ROSY STEWART

Hope: Stories from a Women's Refuge

Cover design by Rosy Stewart

Published by Cricket International

This novel is entirely a work of fiction. The names, characters, and incidents portrayed in it are the work of the author's imagination. Any resemblance to actual persons, living or dead, events, or localities is entirely coincidental.

Anyone affected by these issues may find useful links at our website http://slarner5.wix.com/hope

DEDICATION

To all the victims of domestic violence, and the organisations worldwide who offer their support.

Contents

Prologue

As Liz lay awake in the early hours, she thought of how Viktor had insisted on having sex. Although she had hated every moment she wondered if she had shown too much of an interest tonight. Would he suspect something was different this time?

Viktor seemed to have fallen asleep quickly in the darkness, but Liz had not. As she listened to the autumn rain pattering against the bedroom window, she remembered Sue's words urging her to come back to the Women's Refuge if he was violent again. Liz still felt the pain of bruises from the previous night. She must go now if she wanted to be safe. This was her last chance for a new life.

Viktor's foot was over her ankle, so she would have to slide her leg away very carefully.

She inched away from him, then froze and listened. He was a light sleeper, and his breathing usually responded to any slight movement of hers. But the rhythm did not change.

She reached the edge of the bed and gradually sat up. Once her feet touched the floor, she eased herself up so that there would be no sound from the mattress springs.

She crept around the bed in the dark, guessing its dimensions and pausing after each step to check Viktor's breathing.

Then she slowly opened the bedroom door and quietly closed it behind her.

She tiptoed down the stairs in the dark.

When she reached the hall, she opened the cupboard under the stairs and carefully lifted the lid of the fuse box. There was just enough light to count along the switches to the one that controlled the outside security light. She flicked it to the off position. There was a quiet snap as she closed the fuse box. She waited to hear if there was any sound from upstairs. None.

Liz's heart pounded as she moved across the kitchen, picked up her small rucksack, then turned the key in the back door as slowly as she could. After what seemed like an eternity, she stepped over the threshold. Carefully and silently, she closed the door behind her.

The security light did not come on.

She hurried out into the damp September night, across the wet lawn, avoiding the gravel path, towards her car parked halfway up the street.

The rain ran down her face and into her eyes as she desperately rummaged in her rucksack. There wasn't much there: just a change of clothes, bankcards, a little cash and her passport.

'Please, God, no!' Liz gasped as it dawned on her. For all her planning, in the anxiety of her bid for freedom, she had forgotten to pick up the car key from its usual place on the kitchen shelf.

Now she must face the unthinkable: to go back inside that house. She shivered at the thought. Finally, she brushed the wet hair from her eyes and steeled herself.

Looking up at the windows, she gave a sigh of relief when she saw no light had come on. She retraced her steps over the small garden lawn and approached the back door. Her shoes squelched in the rain-soaked grass.

She waited outside, listening for any noise in the house before putting the key in the lock.

Liz hardly dared to breathe as she opened the door. The kitchen was pitch-black. She felt her way around using the familiar work surfaces as a guide, and stretched her hand up to the shelf to feel for the car key. It was not there!

She thought she heard a noise, a creak. Terrified, she froze and waited. But there was nothing further. The antique Russian wooden furniture that they had collected clicked as it cooled at night in this old house, particularly the sideboard in the hall. She had heard it many times when she had been trying to sleep.

Then there was another noise, almost like the furniture click, but louder and closer, not from the direction of the hall. It came from behind her.

'Are you looking for something?' Viktor enquired in his Russian accent. Liz knew all too well the menace in his tone. The calm control before the rage.

Viktor turned the light on, and as he strode towards her she could see the hatred in his eyes. She raised her arm to shield her head as she braced herself for the inevitable. A fist to her face brought searing pain. Blows to her body made her crumple and finally fall to the kitchen floor. She felt Viktor kick her time after time until everything went black.

Nina's Story

Despite just getting over the flu, Sue was determined to tidy up her office. She vacuumed the worn, brown rug. Even though she was the refuge manager, she liked to do this from time to time. She could at least put some order into a place where so many traumatised women and children had told their terrible stories.

Highburne Refuge was a large end-terraced house in an East London suburb. It was on four levels. The office was in the basement, the residents' lounge and kitchen were on the ground floor, residents' bedrooms on the first floor, and at the top of the building was Sue's self-contained flat.

Sue picked up a small pink teddy bear from the office floor and smiled to herself as she briefly held it close. She brushed away strands of her mousey hair as she bent down and gently laid the teddy bear back in the toy box.

Children who came to the refuge were traumatised. Often they would not be able to talk to adults about their feelings, but they would open up to the pink teddy bear.

Sue was an experienced manager. She had worked eight years at the refuge. Previously she had been a field social worker. But her first experience of a women's refuge had been in a very different role. She had gone into a refuge to escape her own violent partner. It was there that she came to know the power of sharing experiences with other women. Now she was committed to paying back all that help.

The telephone rang. She lifted the phone and answered, 'Sue Barlow...How can I help you?'

She immediately recognised the voice on the other end. It was Police Sergeant Jade Norton. Sue waited for the usual request of a bed for a new police referral to the refuge.

Instead Jade said, 'Sue, I'm afraid I've got some bad news. It's about Liz.'

Jade had supported Liz over the past few months. She had repeatedly advised her to leave Viktor and start a new life from the refuge.

Sue and Jade had become good friends despite the age difference. Jade was in her thirties, ten years younger than Sue. They met regularly for coffee and Sue had been able to confide in Jade about her own experiences of abuse. In turn, Jade was able to speak about the injustice she came across every day in her work as a police officer.

Sue held onto the mantelpiece to steady herself as she listened.

'I'm sorry ... Liz was very badly injured last night. She's in a coma. She's had to be sedated because of a spinal injury and broken ribs. I'm afraid the outlook isn't good.'

'What? How did it happen?'

'She was attacked.'

'Where?'

'In her kitchen. She had a rucksack packed for an overnight stay. Was she on her way to you?'

'Maybe she was,' Sue said. 'I told her that there would always be a place for her here if ever she needed it.'

'There were no signs of a break-in. Of course, we're looking for Viktor, her partner. Have you seen him?'

'No.'

'You don't know where he could have gone?'

'No. Oh Jade, we tried to tell her, didn't we? It's only a month since she left here and went back to him.'

'And if only we could have got Viktor to trial after he kicked her downstairs last year, I reckon he would have been sent down for years. But in the end, she changed her story. She said it was an accident, said it was her own fault.'

'Viktor was such a brute,' Sue snapped. 'Liz was terrified of him.'

'But she always caved in when he said it would never happen again. Look, I'm sorry I can't talk much now, Sue. I've got to dash out to interview Liz's parents. They're at her bedside. Naturally, they're devastated. They're looking after Liz's two kids. I'll pop round to see you this evening and I'll tell you some more.'

Stunned, Sue put the phone down. As she turned towards the mirror above the fireplace her shocked face stared back at her in disbelief. Jade's news had changed her usually warm and calm appearance. A frown accentuated the lines on her face, showing in detail the outward effects of so many years in caring.

She slumped into the old comfortable armchair in the corner of the office and shut her eyes.

Sue remembered Liz telling her how she had first met Viktor by chance at the Science Museum. She was a young widow then with two small children. He was good-looking, immaculately dressed and charming. The children took to him straight away, as he explained the science of the exhibits and bought them gifts from the museum shop. They had tea together and arranged to meet up again in the Victoria and Albert the next week. More meetings followed. After just a short time, she had fallen under his spell. He seemed perfect in every way.

Liz told Sue that Viktor had taken her in his arms and told her that finally he had found the perfect woman. He had been let down so many times in the past.

Liz was overjoyed and asked Viktor to move in with her.

Her happiness was short-lived.

He became increasingly angry about trivial domestic things. Liz eventually moved to Sue's refuge to escape his escalating violence.

One day last month, she had gone back to her house to pick up some of her things. Viktor had been able to get in. She found him drunk, asleep on the sofa. He hadn't changed his clothes for days. There were empty spirit bottles littered across the lounge. Viktor sobbed, said he was sorry if he had hurt Liz in the past. He really loved her. He swore he would never harm her again.

Against Sue's and Jade's advice, Liz went back to him.

At first, Viktor seemed to control his anger, but soon the violence started again, and this week Liz had told Sue that she had made her mind up to put an end to it and leave him once and for all. Sue had a room at the refuge ready and waiting for her.

She must have been heading for the refuge last night.

Suddenly Sue's eyes flashed open. A surge of anger about the whole lousy business flooded through her. She picked up the nearest thing. It was the "Highburne Refuge Standing Operating Orders". The hefty red ring-file manual hit the opposite wall with a bang. The file split open, showing an array of flow charts, and examples of correctly filled-in forms. What was the use of those mumbo-jumbo rules and procedures, she thought, if things like this were going to happen?

She vowed Viktor would pay if only she could trace him. But Viktor knew how to hide. Sue didn't know where to start if the police couldn't find him.

Then she thought about Nina Romanoff, the woman who had known Viktor in Russia, and who had texted Liz months ago to warn her that Viktor had served time in a Russian prison for serious assault. Liz had never answered those messages.

Perhaps Nina might be able to help her find Viktor.

Sue looked up Nina's number in her office file. She had never met her, only spoken to her on the phone.

'Nina, I've got some bad news.'

'What?' replied Nina in her thick Russian accent.

'It's about Liz Williams, the woman who lived with Viktor. She's in hospital in a coma. Someone attacked her.'

There was silence on the end of the line.

When Nina spoke, her voice was gritty and resolved. 'It is Viktor. Where did it happen?'

'In her house. No signs of forced entry.'

'I knew this would happen. I just knew. I warned you. I warned her. I warned everybody....'

'Look, we both tried to help Liz. The police can't trace Viktor. You might be able to think of something they've missed. We can talk about it. I'm going to come round to see you. It's better in person.'

'No, do not!'

'Yes. I can come in my lunch hour. I've got some time owing and it's quiet in the refuge today.'

'I do not get visitors. I am not ready.'

'Oh, you'll be all right. I'm in my working clothes as well.'

'No, I do not want to trouble you.'

'Look, it feels like you might need some support right now. What's your address?'

'No, really...'

'Yes, really. You're in shock. What's your address?'

Reluctantly, Nina told her.

Sue drove out of the quiet and leafy suburb, and then negotiated traffic on the busy main street. She wondered why Nina had been so reticent. Had it brought back bad memories?

She turned into a network of narrow streets, lined with cheap cars and rusty white vans. She parked in an unfamiliar rundown neighbourhood, got out of her car and double-checked that she had locked it. A couple of teenage lads were kicking a ball about on a patch of waste ground, but they showed no interest in her.

Sue walked past a row of three-storey Victorian terraced houses, most of which had been converted into flats. They were fronted by small weed-filled gardens. When she reached Nina's address, she climbed crumbling stone steps to a green front door. Flakes of paint had peeled away so that she could see streaks of the original red beneath.

There was a column of buttons for the flats. Sue scanned the pencilled white nametags by each one. There it was at the top, N. Romanoff.

She pressed the button and waited. A woman's voice with an Eastern European accent enquired through the intercom, 'Hello, who is it?'

'It's Sue.'

'Come up. I am on the third floor.'

The entry buzzer sounded, and Sue pushed open the door. She found herself in a small dark lobby. The carpet was worn and dirty and there was a bowl of faded plastic flowers on a stained wooden table. Sue wrinkled her nose as she breathed in the smell of damp and settled dust.

There was no lift. She started to climb the dark staircase, pausing briefly at each landing to catch her breath. On the second floor someone opened their door a crack, but quickly shut it again.

When she reached the third floor, she saw there was only one door. She guessed that the flat was originally an attic. The door was ajar, but Sue knocked and waited.

'Hello,' Sue called out, but Nina did not appear. Sue could hear her voice coming from inside the flat but could not quite make out the words. She took it as an invitation to come in, and quietly closed the door behind her.

Sue was surprised to see that the curtains were drawn in this first room. But there was a little sunlight filtering through. Her eyes adjusted to the dim light. The room was large and practically bare, just a table and one old-fashioned dining chair. As Sue walked across the bare polished wooden floorboards to a further open door, she heard an echo of her footsteps.

She paused briefly at the threshold of the next room before she entered. Again, the curtains were drawn but this time the light was bright, coming from an array of four computer screens. It seemed like the flight deck of some gigantic plane from the future. And there seated at the controls with her back to Sue, was the pilot... Nina.

She did not turn around. Her slim back was straight. Perfect posture, thought Sue, who was curiously not unnerved by this strange place and her even stranger reception.

'Please sit down,' Nina gestured to a chair on her right. She still faced her computer screen as she spoke. 'It is good to meet at last. I am sorry I cannot give Russian welcome. I am not prepared for company.'

Sue was amazed to see that Nina wore a black gauze veil that obscured the left side of her face. Sue's first thought was that it was some religious requirement, but she had never seen or heard of any strange half-covering like this.

On one of the screens was a live feed from a street cam. Sue recognised it as Liz's street.

'I track Viktor to here,' said Nina, 'Liz's address is on the mobile phone database. It was lucky that she had registered it properly.'

'How did you manage to get all this?'

'It is a hobby of mine. I hack into surveillance cams. Viktor Aleksandrov is very dangerous. I told Liz that so many times. But she took no notice. Now this has happened. It is terrible.'

Nina clicked on the display and rolled back the time shown on the street webcam to 01.00 that morning. The footage showed Liz leaving the house, stopping after a few steps to check her bag, and then creeping back into the house. Fifteen minutes later they saw Viktor emerge and drive off in his car leaving the back door open and the kitchen light on.

Nina pointed at the screen, 'See, there is Viktor. It is him! We must catch him.'

They watched as Viktor drove away. Then the lights came on in the neighbouring houses. They saw people, who must have heard Liz's screams, emerge onto the street wearing coats hurriedly thrown over their nightclothes.

'Jade Norton, my policewoman friend, is pretty sure it was Viktor,' Sue said. 'But we mustn't jump to conclusions.'

'Huh! Believe me, I know. He did it.'

Nina switched on an Anglepoise lamp by her side and turned around to face Sue full on. She lifted the veil from her face.

'He did this to me,' said Nina. 'With acid.'

It was hard to take in the ruin of what had once been a face. The flesh had been melted, then fused and stretched into a travesty.

Scarred lines marked the edges of the acid damage. Pale patches of skin bordered darker ones. A scab where the skin had been grafted was dark and puckered. Her left eye socket was enlarged because the lower eyelid had dropped. That eye seemed cold and dead. In contrast, the right eye showed the presence of an incisive enquiring mind.

'Oh, Nina, how could anyone do this?' gasped Sue.

'It is hard to believe. When we first met I thought Viktor was so gentle, so loving. I had a boyfriend at that time. He was an older cultured man. He was very good to me. But Viktor swept me off my feet. I went to live with him. Bit by bit I found out what he really was. He was a criminal who had made his money from burglary. He started to hit me almost every day. My old boyfriend Sergei confronted him about it. Viktor said he was sorry, but later he did this to me. Of course, he went to prison...eight years. But it was not enough. I promised myself that when he came out I would track him down. Wherever he was. I would make sure he would never hurt any woman again. And now he has done this to Liz! So, go and tell Jade Norton it definitely is Viktor. I emailed her all the video footage a couple of hours ago. I have ways of getting camera records the police do not know. I have also told her everything about Viktor Aleksandrov.'

As she drove through the traffic on her way back to the refuge, Sue sensed that this was the beginning of something that would change her life. Poor Liz was lying in a coma while her abuser went free and unpunished. Viktor had ruined yet another life. Nina was so badly scarred that she felt she could not leave her flat or even meet people. So many other women had been failed by the conventional system. Victims, who had been physically battered and emotionally damaged. Victims without justice.

A wave of anger surged through Sue and she gripped the steering wheel until her knuckles showed white.

When she got back to the refuge office, she looked at the mark on the wall made by the manual she had thrown. A rulebook could not help. It needed a very different approach.

Maggie's Story

Woman Police Sergeant Jade Norton sat in Sue's office nursing a cup of coffee. She shook her head in frustration and ran her fingers through her short dark hair. The system wasn't working, and Jade had been feeling for some time that one day she would have to bend the rules. This would be counter to her upbringing as her father had been a police inspector.

'We are almost certain it was Viktor who attacked Liz,' she told Sue. 'But we've no idea where he is now. We can't even trace his car. Our team have gone through all the street cams and got no leads. Even the footage that Nina, your Russian IT expert, sent us hasn't thrown anything up. We can only wait for a report of an abandoned or burnt-out Peugeot to come through over the next few days. But by then Viktor will be well away.'

Sue frowned at this news.

There was a pause before Jade added, 'The stuff Nina sent me about her life is tragic. Is it all true?'

'Yes. I've seen her face and it's horrific. No wonder she wants to help track Viktor down.'

'I've looked her up in the records. She approached the police a long time ago, but it wasn't followed up.'

Sue had suspected that might have been the case. She knew all too well important things could be overlooked in a complex administration system.

She glanced at her watch. 'It's almost visiting time at the hospital.'

Jade reached in her jacket for her car keys. 'Let's go!' she said.

The Royal Eastfield Hospital was a huge box-like structure fronted with an array of glass panels that reflected the last rays of the autumn sun.

Jade parked her police car on double yellows near the entrance, making sure to leave room for other vehicles.

The automatic doors led to a large atrium that looked more like the interior of a shopping mall than a hospital.

Sue and Jade followed the signs to the high dependency unit.

A nurse led them to a four-bedded bay at the end of the ward. Two of the beds were empty. A pale, barely conscious older woman was in the third. Sitting on the edge of her bed and holding her hand was someone who might be her daughter. She was still wearing her coat despite the heat of the ward.

The fourth bed had curtains drawn around it.

'You can see her now,' the nurse said, pulling the curtains back from around the bed. 'She's still unconscious, I'm afraid.'

There were stitches around Liz's blackened and bruised face. Bandages covered her scalp and jaw. In the back of her hand was a needle attached to a drip.

Surrounding Liz's bed was a drip-stand, a heart monitor and a suction machine. On a bedside table were photographs of her children, a box of tissues, and a folder containing nursing notes.

When Sue spoke her name, Liz's eyelids flickered but stayed shut.

'Poor thing,' said Jade. 'She looks as though she is going through a nightmare. The nurses say they'll let us know if there's any change, but I don't think there will be for some time.'

They sat with Liz. Sue held her hand, and talked quietly and reassuringly to her. Even though Liz did not respond, Sue felt in her heart that Liz knew they were there and that they cared.

After a quarter of an hour, Sue and Jade left with the flood of people at the end of visiting time, knowing that Liz's parents would soon be back to resume their vigil.

As they walked over to Jade's car, Sue said 'It should never have happened. She was too young. We should have done more to stop it.'

'We did everything we could.'

'Did we? I wonder.'

Jade climbed into the driver's seat of the car and Sue settled down next to her. She took a tissue out of her handbag to wipe away her tears.

'If only I'd gone to visit Liz at home after she left the refuge. But I had to have time off work when I had the flu. I was in bed for days. I'm only just getting over it now.'

'Don't blame yourself, Sue,' Jade comforted. 'You did everything you could. But you know there is another woman at risk we can help this time.'

Sue put aside her tissue. 'Who?'

'Her name's Maggie Smith. She's in hospital at the moment getting over a drugs overdose. She won't tell me much. All I know is that she has been working as a prostitute in Newcastle and she is really frightened of something. She hasn't said what. She's got a baby in care. It would be great if you could have a word with her.'

Sue didn't hesitate for a second. She rummaged around in her large handbag and drew out a small yellow diary and pen. 'I can go tomorrow afternoon. Just let me have the details.'

At visiting time the next afternoon, it was pouring with rain and Sue was late. For what seemed an eternity she had been circling around the car park trying to find a space. Finally, she squeezed in a space by a wall and ran across to the hospital entrance.

She studied the hospital direction signs above the large green double doors. Hawthorne Ward, where Jade had told her she would find Maggie.

The corridor was packed with nurses and visitors bustling back and forth. Sue drew close to a wall as a trolley passed. An elderly woman with a pale expressionless face was lying on it. Sue tried not to look too long and hard.

She was frightened yet fascinated by hospitals. Sue was generally healthy except for her recent flu, but she had received emergency treatment in hospital ten years ago for a broken arm inflicted by her husband. It seemed to her that she had been a different person then. Like Maggie, she too had been a victim living in fear, controlled and abused by a violent man. Now she was free and confident enough to help another woman who might be in a similar situation.

There was a small buzzer next to the doors leading to Hawthorne ward. Sue pressed it and a nurse let her in. Sue explained who she was and was led to one of the side rooms, near the nurses' station.

Sue saw a dark-haired young woman curled up on top of the bed. Her eyes were closed. She was wearing a thin dressing gown. Sue could easily make out the contours of bones protruding from her emaciated body.

'Maggie?' Sue enquired softly.

The young woman opened dark heavily-lashed eyes that dominated her haggard face. She struggled to raise herself slightly on one elbow to study Sue.

'Yes,' she said in a strong Geordie accent. 'Who are you?'

'Sergeant Norton asked me to come and see you. I'm Sue, and I manage a local women's refuge. I know you are not quite ready to leave hospital yet, but I wondered if you would like to stay with us for a while when you are discharged?'

Maggie did not answer. She just fixed Sue with a gaze from dark eyes empty of all emotion.

'You would have time to get things sorted,' Sue said. 'It's a safe place and you would be very welcome.'

Maggie gave a short low laugh. 'A safe place?'

'Well, we've had no unwelcome visitors in the eight years I've been there. Another thing is, we have rooms for mums who have babies. Sergeant Norton told me you have a little boy. How old is he?'

Maggie managed a wistful smile. 'He'll be six months tomorrow.'

'What's his name?'

'Alex.'

'That's a nice name.'

'I expect they'll change it though when he's adopted.'

Sue tried to hide her surprise. 'Is that what you want?' she said.

'No, I don't really, but I've got to do what's best for him.'

'I'm sure you've thought long and hard about it.'

Suddenly Maggie recoiled on the bed. She started to shake, and her face turned ashen. She stared at the partly open side room door.

Sue turned and glimpsed a man's face. He was looking through the doorway into the room. When he saw Sue, he withdrew so quickly that she couldn't register his appearance except that he had black hair.

'They've found me!' Maggie gasped. 'You have to go.'

Sue took a step towards the door and peered out into the corridor, but there was no one there.

'Go now!' said Maggie. 'Quick! You don't know what you're getting into.'

Sue turned to face Maggie. 'I can come tomorrow if you like.'

'No, don't do that!'

Sue realised that Maggie was so upset and agitated that staying to talk would only make things worse.

She swiftly said goodbye and retraced her path to the hospital lobby.

It was still raining outside, though not as heavily as before. She walked slowly and thoughtfully across the car park.

What was happening? Surely the man who had looked into Maggie's room was just a visitor trying to find his friend or relative. It was quite natural because all those rooms looked the same. Yet Maggie had reacted in such an extreme way. Perhaps there was something more to this than prostitution. Could money be involved? Maybe a drugs debt?

'Don't be silly,' Sue thought. 'You're just letting your imagination get the better of you.'

She rummaged for her car key that inevitably had

worked its way down to the very bottom of her large, packed handbag. As she did so, she noticed a man standing beside a nearby black car. He tilted his umbrella so that she couldn't see his face.

As she drove away, Sue checked her rear mirror. The black car was following her.

She made a sudden turn, but the black car kept on her tail. Scared by this, she drove into town and circled around. Finally, she was able to jump some traffic lights and make a sharp turn into a maze of streets. She parked and waited, frozen with fear.

Sue was anxious to drive off, but she decided to be safe and give it another ten minutes before edging back into the traffic.

There was no sign of the black car. She weaved her way along the busy high street to the refuge. She parked some spaces down the road so as not to give away its location.

Once safely inside her flat at the top of the refuge she made herself a coffee. She found that her hands were shaking.

After a few sips, she steadied her hands and phoned Jade.

'Jade, I was followed after I visited Maggie in the hospital.'

'How do you know?'

'It was a man in a black car, but I managed to shake him off.'

'Hang on, this might be significant. I'll be there in about twenty minutes. Then we can go back to the hospital together.'

When they returned to the hospital, Jade parked the police car near the back entrance of the accident and emergency department.

Waiting patients looked up as Sue and Jade walked through reception, but a shifty burly man in a suit looked down at his newspaper.

Sue felt that he was rather like the man who had followed her, but she couldn't be sure.

Sue and Jade waited at the nursing station in Hawthorne Ward. There was a doctor with his back to them who was studying X-Rays. He was dressed casually in check cotton shirt and brown trousers. His shirtsleeves were rolled up. He had a stethoscope around his neck and an ID badge clipped to a trouser pocket. He seemed intent on what he was doing, and they did not want to interrupt him.

Presently a nurse came up to the station with some papers, and snapped them into a ring folder on the counter. She wore navy blue, and her brown hair was tied into a bun.

Jade recognised her from the day before. 'Hi, Sam, any change in Maggie Smith?'

'No. Just the same. Pretending to be asleep whenever you go near her, but really watching everything. She's taken some fluids, but not eaten.'

'OK to go in?'

'Sure, but I don't think you'll get anything out of her.'

'Well. I doubt whether she'll co-operate with me if she won't with you.' Then Jade added as she turned away, 'But I'll try my best.'

Sue and Jade walked down to Maggie's side room.

Inside, Maggie seemed asleep. She had dark rings around her sunken eyes.

She opened them and looked at Sue in a dreamy, half-conscious way.

Then she stared past them through the open doorway.

Her eyes widened in terror. She muttered, 'No. No... Don't let him come in here.'

Instantly Jade left the room to check the corridor.

Maggie squirmed in the bed, her breathing quickened. One arm seemed to be fighting off some imaginary person, the other clutched the mattress as she tried to hoist herself out of the bed.

'Hey, calm down,' Sue reassured Maggie. 'We're friends. We're here to help.'

After a short time, Jade came back into the room. 'There's no one there,' she said.

Maggie sank back onto the bed.

'You've just had a bad dream,' Jade reassured her. 'That's all.'

As Sue touched Maggie's arm to try to calm her, she saw the pinpricks and the scars left by needles.

'How long have you been using?' she asked.

'Just a couple of times.' Maggie looked at the window to avoid Sue's gaze.

'No. We both know it's more than that.'

Maggie shouted, 'He's here! Don't let him get me!'

'Who?' asked Sue.

'Him. I saw him today and yesterday.'

'Where?'

'Out there!' She pointed in the direction of the ward lounge.

Despite Jade's further questioning, Maggie clammed up and she wouldn't say any more.

Sue left her mobile number with the nursing staff in case Maggie decided she would like to stay at the refuge when she was discharged.

Sue and Jade left the hospital together. In accident and emergency reception, the shifty-looking man with the newspaper had gone.

As they returned to Jade's car, Sue had the feeling once again that they were being followed. She looked back, but there was no one there. She put it down to the shock of her strange interaction with Maggie.

'You've seen too many American cop films.' Jade laughed, catching Sue glancing back as they drove out of the hospital car park. 'Mind you the villains will have to watch out now that you have done that self-defence training.'

'Well, Social Services said we all had to go on the course. It gave me more confidence, but I don't think I'll ever be a martial arts expert.'

The journey back to the refuge was uneventful.

While Sue was making herself a cup of coffee in her flat, she thought about Maggie and what a sad life she had. It was going to be almost impossible to help her if she wouldn't open up.

Then she had a flash of inspiration. If Maggie had spent time working the streets of Newcastle, perhaps she had been caught on CCTV. Nina might be able to tap into street cam records for any images of her with suspect characters.

She rang Nina.

'I am trying to find some information about a woman called Maggie Smith and I wondered if you can help. She is dark-haired, about 20, five feet five and very thin. She is a heroin user and worked the streets in Newcastle.'

'OK,' said Nina. 'I will try for images. I will send them. You can see if she is in them.'

After a short while, Sue's computer beeped and some files appeared attached to an email. Sue opened them.

She was able to exclude some immediately. One woman was much older than Maggie, and another had a hood obscuring her face. One of the pictures showed a dark-haired woman of Maggie's age talking to a group of other women. Even though she had her back to the camera, Sue could see from her skimpy clothing and her bare legs that this was not the emaciated girl in the hospital.

Then she saw a thin girl of around twenty wearing high heels, caught on camera standing in a doorway.

'There's one here that certainly looks like her,' Sue emailed back.

Nina agreed to search further databases and to find out if Maggie had appeared on other street cams.

After a little while, Nina pinpointed the area where Maggie had worked. In some of the earlier images, she looked pregnant as well.

Nina also sent images of men from the street cams – not necessarily punters, but probably pimps from the way they were interacting with Maggie: getting money from her, then giving her small sachets.

Sue phoned Nina.

'These look good. Can you find some clearer pictures of these men?'

'I will try. I can search street and shop cameras, more than police can. If the cameras send wirelessly to their hosts, then I break the encryption codes. It is not legal of course, but what is out in the airwaves is, as you say in English, fair game.' Nina paused, and then said thoughtfully, 'I can see already there is someone who talks much with Maggie. He appears a lot in bars. I had a scare for a minute. It looked a bit like Viktor, but I can see now it was not him.'

As Sue opened the file, she gasped as she immediately recognised the burly man who had been in the accident and emergency waiting room.

Sue relayed this to Jade, taking care to disguise the source of information since it was technically stolen. She was relieved when Jade didn't question her further and just said, 'OK. I'll put a watch on the hospital, and wait for him to show up again. I'll meet you there the same time tomorrow. Perhaps Maggie will open up then.'

That night Sue had difficulty sleeping and thought she heard noises at the back of the refuge. Was it an intruder? She discounted this and put it down to her imagination. She tossed and turned, thinking about Liz and Maggie.

Next afternoon Sue arrived early at the hospital, but Jade had phoned to say she would be delayed. Nevertheless, Sue went straight to Hawthorne ward.

As she left the nursing station and walked down the corridor to Maggie's side room, she saw a man heading up towards her. She recognised him from the Newcastle images.

'Excuse me, can I help you?' she asked intercepting him as he came up to a trolley laden with cups and a large metal teapot. But he merely grunted, dismissed her with a wave of his hand and tried to continue on his path.

With a quick side-step, Sue got in front of him and demanded, 'Who are you?'

Attracted by Sue's loud voice, Maggie peered out around the door of her side room.

The man tried to elbow Sue out of the way to get to Maggie. Sue could hardly believe what was happening, but she flared up and reacted with one of the moves she had learned at self-defence. She kicked behind his ankle and pushed him back. He fell against the wall.

Seconds later, he recovered and came back at her. Sue grabbed the tea trolley and steered it towards him, shoving it into his stomach. The loud clatter of falling cups and saucers alerted nurses up the corridor.

He pushed the trolley back towards Sue. Then he drew out a knife.

Sue saw the glint of the blade as he lunged towards her. She instinctively picked up the large metal teapot from the trolley and threw it at him.

As the hot water hit his face, he howled in agony and dropped the knife.

The noise brought the nurses and a security guard rushing. They pinned the attacker to the floor.

Sue stood there in horror watching the struggle, and a few minutes later Jade arrived to make the arrest.

Jade and Sue came to comfort Maggie as she half-collapsed in shock in her doorway, having witnessed it all.

She stared at Sue. 'That was amazing. I'd no idea anybody could stand up to someone like that.'

'I just did it without thinking,' Sue said. 'We don't always have to be victims.'

'He can't hurt you now, Maggie,' said Jade. 'So, do you want to tell us about him?'

Maggie had become addicted to drugs through her boyfriend. After some time, he had told her that the only way for her to get money for drugs was to go into prostitution.

She worked for a gang in Newcastle, but had run away to London because she was frequently beaten up by her pimps. She became terrified not only for herself, but also for her newborn baby.

The gang had followed Maggie to London. They had injected her with an overdose and left her for dead as a warning to other women who might also try to escape.

When she woke up in hospital, she thought people were out to get her. The nurses had tried to reason with her, telling her that she must be confused from the drugs. Then her worst fears were confirmed when she saw the leader of the gang peering into her side room.

She was terrified to speak to anyone and had spent days in hospital in fear of her life, convinced no one could help her and her son.

Maggie was now more than happy to take up Sue's offer of a place in the refuge. She intended to testify against the gang leader who had tried to kill her. It was likely he would receive a lengthy prison sentence.

Best of all, after input from Social Services and the drug rehabilitation team she would be able to have her baby son Alex returned to her in the near future.

Before she left the hospital, Sue decided to call in to see Liz. It had broken her heart to see this lovely young woman cheated of her future. As she sat talking to her, she thought she saw a flicker of her eyelids and a slight movement of her fingers as if she was aware. But the doctors were not at all optimistic. The injuries that Viktor had inflicted were so severe. Sue worried how long the hospital would want to continue caring for Liz if she showed no signs of recovery in the near future.

'We can only hope that time will heal her,' Sue reflected to a nurse on leaving the ward. 'Each time I come I'll tell her about how we have helped other women at the refuge. She might not be able to speak, but I believe she is listening and will understand.'

The ward door closed automatically behind her.

A few days later as Sue and Jade entered Liz's ward, they received some encouraging news. The sedation had been reduced, and Liz would soon begin to come out of her coma. She might then be moved into one of the side rooms for less dependent patients.

'I'll come in with you,' the nurse said, 'because I need to check on her.'

As soon as they entered the room, they greeted Liz who opened her eyes.

Sue and Jade cried out with surprise and delight.

Liz's head was still but her eyes tracked all around the room, puzzled as if she had never seen anything like that before.

The nurse said, 'That's great – how are you, Liz?'

She did not speak, but just moved her eyes to one side.

The nurse said, 'This is a very promising sign and we can build on it. It's early days yet but there are lots of practical ways you can really help her.'

'Tell us what to do and we'll do it,' said Sue.

'Call her by name every time you come in and go out. Keep what you say simple and short. Encourage her to look at you. Give her time, and always give her loads of praise.'

Sue and Jade smiled at each other knowing that now they were on the right track.

Rula's Story

S ue was driving to a meeting at Social Services head office when her mobile rang.

She pulled over.

It was Nina.

'Hi, Sue,' said Nina. 'I have found an unusual comment on my website.'

'You get those all the time. What's different about this one?'

'It is in code. It is very strange. If it is true, then someone could use your help. Are you near the north side of town?'

'Look, Nina, I'm on my way to a meeting about the refuge project.'

'Well, this will not take a minute. It sounds desperate.'

'How so?'

'It is written in an old Polish war code. No one uses this now. Decoded, it says: "I am trapped, Rula. Linden House." '

'Linden House?'

'Yes. It is off Westmoreland Road. In the avenues at the back. Ah….' Nina paused.

Sue could hear clicking on a computer keyboard, as Nina continued, 'I can see your location. You are not far.'

Sue groaned. Though it was very useful at times for Nina to be able to track her location, there were occasions when she'd rather not be available.

'It is important, Sue,' Nina pleaded. 'This person sounds in big trouble.'

Sue looked at her watch, and then up and down the street. Westmoreland Road was just ahead on the left.

'OK. I'll have a quick look. I've only got a few minutes, though.'

'That will be enough.'

Sue followed the sat-nav to Linden House. It wasn't far off her route – just a few easy turns into wide leafy avenues. She pulled up opposite the overgrown driveway of a large late Victorian house set in grounds of mature oak and dark laurel. The house was on three storeys with a drive extending around the back. It had two massive sash bay windows at the front with red frames. The front lawn was overdue for cutting. Nearer to the house was an empty concrete pond with a crumbling stone statue of a water nymph set in its middle.

Sue decided to walk rather than drive up to the house, so she would not attract attention. It was eerie and quiet with no signs of life, but Sue had an uneasy feeling that she was being watched.

She had already thought of an excuse to justify her unannounced visit. She carried a huge teddy bear that had been donated with other bric à brac to the refuge by a local nursery. It had been in the boot of her car for over a week. The teddy bear had blue fur and alarming orange glass eyes. The little children who came to the nursery were usually terrified when it was brought out for them to play with. But now, Sue had another use for it.

At the top of three stone steps was an old oak door. She pressed the antique circular bell to the right of the door. As the bell rang, a dog barked in the back of the house.

No one answered. She rang again. Then a third time. Just as she had decided to give up and to try to find another door, it was opened by a sombrely-dressed middle-aged woman. Her long brown hair was combed back and pinned into a severe pleat. She had a pale angular face and etched lines around her eyes that gave her the appearance of having a permanent frown.

'Yes?' The woman enquired in a far from friendly manner.

'Oh, good morning,' Sue smiled. 'Are you Rula by any chance?'

'No, I'm not,' the woman replied frostily. 'What do you want?'

'Well this is the address I have for a lady called Rula. She's won this in our charity raffle.' Sue held the teddy bear out for inspection. 'It was an online raffle, but I thought as I live near you I could just pop it in myself. Have I got the right house?'

'It could be for my employer. I'm the housekeeper. I'll see she gets it. Thank you.'

The housekeeper took the bear and began to close the door, but Sue quickly said, 'Oh I forgot to say, she just has to sign this form to say she has received her prize.'

The housekeeper's face became even more disapproving.

'That's not possible. The Countess is indisposed, and she is not able to have visitors. I think you better take this back. We wouldn't have any need of it here.' Saying this, she thrust the bear back into Sue's arms and slammed the door in her face.

Within seconds, it was flung open again to reveal the hulking figure of a man. He was at least six feet four. He wore a waistcoat over a white shirt with rolled-up sleeves. His piercing dark eyes seemed to bore into Sue, and instinctively she backed away.

'What's this? What do you want?' he barked.

'I'm sorry. All I wanted was a signature for this,' Sue held out the teddy bear.

'Countess Malinowska is not well,' said the man. 'And she can't talk to you. Thank you. Goodbye.'

Then, abruptly, he closed the door in Sue's face.

Dismissed, and remembering the need to get on with her day's work, she walked briskly back down the drive. She shrugged her shoulders, and dumped the teddy bear in the boot of her car.

Before setting off, Sue pressed the speed-dial button to Nina.

'Well?' Nina asked. 'That was quick.'

'They didn't want to see me.'

'OK. No matter. Perhaps a false alarm.'

'Probably,' Sue said, signing off the phone and muttering to herself thoughtfully 'Or maybe not.'

As she drove off Sue was still reeling from her reception at that front door. She tapped on the steering wheel and frowned. She had seen negative initial responses before. The loud denial of a family, or the strange calculating smoothness of an accomplished liar. However, this was something different. A very uncompromising angry response.

A few days later Sue was in her office when she got another call from Nina.

'They have sent the message again.'

'Well, I think we should get the police involved now. I'll ask Jade. I've been there once and they didn't let me in. I got the feeling they won't want me to come back.'

Sue rang Jade who asked immediately, 'How do we know it's not a hoax?'

'For one thing, they sound desperate. Nina managed to get a trace on the iphone at the time that they sent this message. It's definitely from inside the house.'

'It might be people mucking about. Perhaps children?'

'I'm sure it isn't. How's it going to look if the police decide not to investigate, and at the end of the day it turns out to be a murder enquiry?'

Jade paused before replying. 'We're hard pushed at the moment, Sue, but I'll try to send the community constable round. Maybe they'll have better luck getting inside.'

A couple of days later Jade rang Sue back.

'The community constable said there wasn't any problem. There's lots of servants working there. It was like an episode of Downton. A butler character ushered the constable into the drawing room. It was incredible. Chandeliers hanging from really high ceilings... long velvet curtains...Chinese carpets, all the wooden furniture polished so you could see your face in it. Honestly, the constable was frightened to sit down or touch anything. Anyway, the butler was very polite.'

'A bit different from when I spoke to him,' Sue interrupted.

'He called the housekeeper in. That must have been the woman you spoke to at the door. She was pleasant enough and answered all the constable's questions. It seems that Rula, Countess Malinowska, stays in her room most of the time. She is an invalid and confused at times. The butler, George, showed the constable all the prescription tablets she is taking. They had her name on them. George gave the constable the mobile number of the community nurse who visits Rula and he confirmed what was happening. He was a bit worried about confidentiality, but understood it was important the police knew the truth about Rula's condition. He felt she could easily have sent a message to say she was being held prisoner when she was in one of her confused states. Anyway, I think they were pleased to know she was sending those emails, so they could watch out for her doing it again. She seems to be very well looked after. I wish I had a house and a few servants like her.'

Sue went to bed feeling much happier now she knew the truth about Rula. It did seem very unlikely that a person would be held prisoner in this day and age, especially someone who was obviously wealthy and could afford to employ servants. However, all the same, Sue felt sorry for Rula. Money had not been able buy her health and peace of mind.

The next morning Sue woke early and refreshed. She was looking forward to it being her day off. Cath, her deputy, could deal with the piles of paperwork that the refuge increasingly had to produce to get funding.

She dressed and put her coat on. It was a blustery autumn morning and rain was on the way. Sue planned to go up to town first thing, just as the shops were opening, to buy some winter clothes. However, as she was locking the door to her flat on the top floor of the refuge, her mobile rang.

'It is Nina. I have just had another message, a few

minutes ago from a phone in Rula's home. This time it is from a new maid at the house. Her name is Lucy. She says the policeman who called yesterday got tricked by the butler and the housekeeper. It is all lies. Rula really is a prisoner and she is in terrible danger. George the butler suspects we know what is going on.'

Sue immediately rang Jade to tell her about this third message, but Jade still refused to act, saying there was no evidence that anything was wrong when the community constable had visited. She said that he would go again next week to tie up any loose ends. She finished by saying, 'Don't do anything silly like breaking in, because that would be an offence, and you could be prosecuted.'

Jade ended the call, leaving Sue's mind churning. This is what happens when you have to follow the rules. People are put at risk to protect the system. Sometimes you should follow your instincts.

She was interrupted by her phone. It was Nina.

'I have another message from Lucy. Rula must be rescued today. Soon she will be too weak, because of her ill treatment.'

'But how?' Sue asked. 'The place is swarming with servants. It sounds like they are all involved.'

'Yes, it could be dangerous,' Nina agreed. 'But as you say in English, nothing ventured nothing gained. I can guide you in by phone. Head for the back cellar window. Lucy will be there waiting for you when she gets my call.'

'When should I go?' Sue asked nervously.

'Now,' Nina replied. 'It could be a matter of life or death. Lucy gave me some family details. I am trying to contact them for a video call. Then they can talk directly to Rula.'

Once again, Sue parked her car on the road close to the entrance of the drive leading to Linden House.

For a few seconds her hands gripped the wheel, steeling herself for the task ahead before she finally got out.

She couldn't see any sign of surveillance cameras on the gates. She studied the garden before she walked in. Her plan was to quickly get off the main pathway and head for the trees to her left. Nina had examined satellite images of the house and gardens and she had told Sue that the wooded section of the grounds curved around to the back of the house.

Sue heard Nina's voice through her earphones. 'When you come out of the wood you will see the low windows that go down to the lawn. They lead to the cellar. Go to the third one on your right. Lucy will be there to let you in. I have located Rula's family. They live in Poland and they know now she is ill and being held captive by George. They are appalled. They will stand by their phone and we can video conference with Rula once you get to her.'

Sue's heart pounded as she walked quickly into the wood that fringed the garden. It was dark and quiet in there and Sue couldn't believe what she was doing. Once she felt sure that no one would be able to see her from the house, she spoke to Nina. 'I'm here,' she said. 'I'm frightened to death, though.'

'You are doing just great,' Nina reassured her. 'This is for Rula, remember.'

Sue took some deep breaths to try to relax, and then started to walk through the woods to the side of the house. The leaves on the ground cushioned the sound of her footsteps. From time to time, she stopped to listen if there was anyone else nearby. Suddenly she heard a rustle and jumped in alarm. It was only a bird she had disturbed.

She resumed her slow careful progress until she saw the house through the trees. It looked even larger from the back and appeared quite forbidding.

When she reached the edge of the trees, Sue saw a stretch of freshly-cut grass in front of her at the side of the house. Now there was no hiding from anyone who might be looking out of the upper windows, but she thought it was such a short distance to the cellar window she would make a dash for it. Sue started to move out of cover, but then she heard a loud whirring sound. To her horror, around the corner of the house, a man on a motor mower was coming in her direction.

She darted back to hide behind a tree, and held her breath as she waited to see if he had noticed her. Gradually the whirring sound became fainter. Sue realised he was cutting the grass in a circuit of the house and was now at the front. She would have time to run across the grass and get through the cellar window providing Lucy the maid was there to let her in.

It was now or never. With her heart in her mouth, Sue raced across the lawn. As she got near the third window, she saw it was closed and she couldn't see anyone inside.

She flattened herself against the window and started to tap on it. Then, inevitably, she heard the faint sound of the motor mower returning on its circular path. The sound grew louder. It was too late to run back to the woods for cover. Sue turned around racking her brains for some feeble excuse to explain her inevitable discovery. Suddenly she felt a pressure against her back. Someone was opening the window behind her.

Sue heard a voice 'Quick!', and she grasped an outstretched hand. She summoned all her strength to scramble through the open cellar window. She landed on a cold stone floor. Lucy closed the window and helped Sue to her feet.

'Are you Sue?' Lucy whispered. She was a pretty woman in her late twenties, well spoken and dressed in a smart suit. She did not fit Sue's picture of a lady's maid.

'Yes. You must be Lucy. Is Rula ready to leave?'

'Yes, she knows she's in danger now. George the butler has got all the servants under his thumb. They've worked for him in this place for a year, and help him to keep Rula a prisoner.'

'So, how did all this come about?'

'He wormed his way into her life after her husband died. Rula emigrated from Poland and the Count, her husband, passed away almost as soon as they got here. She couldn't speak English so George said he would manage all her affairs. She came to depend on him for everything. I think he wanted to marry her but she must have sensed he was just after her money.'

'How did he manage to keep her a prisoner?'

'He drugs her by overdosing her with her own medication. When she is confused they get her to write and sign letters telling her relatives that she's happy but cannot leave the house to visit them. The so-called Community Nurse the constable phoned was just the head gardener. I've only worked here for a couple of days and I've pretended to go along with George's plan.'

Warning Sue to be quiet, Lucy led her up a winding staircase at the back of the house that led to an attic room. Lucy got out a key and unlocked the door.

Rula, who was sleeping on a single bed, stirred awake when the two women entered. Sue was horrified at how starved and pale she looked. Rula was too weak even to speak.

Sue phoned Nina, who connected her via video to Rula's family in Poland.

They were distraught to see the state that Rula was in. They had already been alerted by Nina and were at the airport ready to board the next flight from Warsaw to rescue her.

Lucy reassured Sue that she would look after Rula until her family arrived as she helped Sue back out of the cellar window. Sue crept out and into the wood, carefully avoiding the gardener.

Later that same day, Lucy rang Sue to let her know that the relatives were on their way from Heathrow to Linden House.

Sue remembered that Jade had told her not to get involved, so she just watched from a distance in her parked car in the avenue. Three men and three women got out of two taxis and burst into the house past Lucy who had been outside waiting to meet them.

Half an hour later, the relatives emerged and bundled the now-haggard butler into a waiting car.

The rest of the staff followed except for Lucy. Sue wondered what had happened to her and was afraid that Rula's rescuers might have mistakenly assaulted her. She cautiously made her way into the house.

She found Lucy sitting with Rula in the lounge. Rula was supported by pillows in an armchair. All the staff had been sacked and the family were still thinking about how they would deal with George the butler.

Rula weakly held out her hand to Sue. In a voice full of emotion she said, 'Bless you for what you have done. You have saved my life. I'll never forget this.'

Lucy said. 'She will be safe now. Her family have asked me to stay and look after her.'

A few weeks after Rula's rescue, Sue had a phone call from Lucy asking if they could meet up for tea in the Dorchester Hotel.

Sue was more accustomed to having a quick coffee in her local supermarket café than a five-star hotel, but she agreed. The rescue had been so dramatic and she couldn't wait to hear the conclusion to Rula's story.

Sue had her hair done specially and was wearing her best clothes as she entered the hotel lounge, with its plush carpets and marble columns. In the past she would have felt self-conscious and out of place, but now she walked in confidently, flushed with her recent success.

Lucy waved to her from a table across the room. She had ordered tea, and accompanying the china pot and white gold-rimmed teacups was a silver stand holding delicate sandwiches and prettily-decorated cakes. They were served by a waiter wearing white gloves.

'It's good to see you,' Lucy smiled. 'A bit different from our first meeting when you fell in the cellar window?'

Sue laughed and settled herself down on a comfortable cushioned chair at the table.

They chatted about everyday things, and then Lucy said, 'You know I thought you would like to hear the happy ending that Rula and I have to thank you for. We live in town now, quite near to here. I suppose you could say this was our 'local'. I'm doing my Sociology PhD and Rula is developing her English. She would have come today, but she's flown out to Poland to spend some time with her family. She has lots of relatives. When they heard what had happened to her they were so angry. Some of her cousins were for quietly doing away with George, but Rula persuaded them not to. She's a very kind woman. Yet the family gave George a choice. He could stay in the UK and be prosecuted for theft and unlawful imprisonment, or he could return to Poland and work as a servant for Rula's Uncle. He has a castle, but George will find the position they have offered him is not as a butler...it's as the stable boy. I think he has to sleep in the stable with the horses, and I believe it's very, very cold in that part of the country.'

When Sue and Lucy had finished tea, they said their

goodbyes and agreed to meet again the next month when Rula could join them. Then they would hear news of how George was settling into his new and humbler lifestyle.

'Rula wants you to have this,' Lucy said as they parted. She handed her a carrier bag inside which was a tough cardboard box. Sue opened the box, and inside was a beautiful blue vase.

'That's only a little present for you personally, but the main present is this. It's for the refuge.' Lucy handed Sue an embossed pale blue envelope.

Sue carefully opened the envelope. Inside was a card written in copperplate, 'With my love, and my thanks that no words can express. Please use this small token to continue your wonderful work with women who need your help.'

Sue could not believe her eyes as she stared at the amount on the cheque made out in her name.

With tears of happiness in her eyes, she murmured 'Thank you, Rula. It will be put to good use, I promise you.'

On her next visit to see Liz in hospital, Sue found that she had been moved into a side room. Sue was able to tell her about Rula and the wonderful gift she had given the refuge. Liz showed excitement at hearing this news, though Sue wasn't convinced she had understood everything.

Although Liz was sitting up she couldn't speak much and often she drifted to sleep. She was able to recognise family and friends, but would easily get exhausted and confused.

She needed help with dressing and walking to the bathroom. Sue saw how frustrated she became when unable to do ordinary things like pulling a dressing gown around her shoulders.

As Sue recounted more of the Rula story, Liz's eyes closed and she dozed off.

Sue looked at the bedside table. There was a photo of her parents and her two children taken on a family outing to the zoo. A small alarm clock in the shape of a Teddy Bear stood alongside a plastic wallet containing a sheet of this week's plan of activities including physiotherapy and occupational therapy.

A knock on the side room door interrupted Sue's story. A nurse came in. Liz opened her eyes.

'Hi, I wonder if you can help me. We just need to update Liz's notes. Is it still the same next of kin? We've got Viktor Aleksandrov down.'

Liz froze. Her eyes opened wide. She gave out a low cry, shook in terror and tried to raise herself in the bed. The cry got louder. 'No. No. No!'

She sank back onto the pillow and collapsed in tears.

Paula's Story

Mornings were chaotic in the refuge. Women queued for the bathroom in their dressing gowns; babies were being changed and fed; older children were shouted at to get dressed and have breakfast in time for school. It was not surprising that sometimes tempers were frayed.

Paula, a new resident, had occupied the first-floor bathroom for over twenty minutes. Outside two women were grumbling to each other.

'How long does it take to have a quick wash?' asked Gilly, with a towel under her arm and a wash bag in her hand. 'I can be in and out in five minutes.'

Another large woman in a dressing gown standing next to her in the queue knocked on the door and shouted through it. 'There's people waiting out here. Are you going to be all day?'

After a few seconds, Paula slowly opened the bathroom door. She was fully dressed and had done her hair and makeup.

The two women who were waiting did not speak, but glared at Paula as she came out of the bathroom.

'Sorry,' Paula whispered as she scurried with lowered eyes back to her single room.

Sue, and Cath her deputy, thought that Paula was a bit of an oddity too. She hardly ever spoke to anyone except when she had to. She seemed to be well-educated, and her appearance was always immaculate. Such qualities were not usually admired in the refuge.

No one knew much about Paula's background except that she worked at a nursery and that she was on leave of absence for a few weeks, after separating from an abusive partner.

Sometimes Paula seemed terribly sad and she would fight to hold back tears. Then she would leave the refuge and could be away for several hours. No one knew where she went or what she did.

However, there was one thing about Paula that the women at the Refuge really valued: she was wonderful with little children. It seemed she had a natural gift. She could soothe any screaming infant in seconds, and when she sat down on the lounge floor all the pre-school children would gather around her as she engaged them in play.

Paula was in her thirties with freckles and ginger hair. Her gaunt face became animated whenever she communicated with young children and perhaps that was why they liked her so much. Her smile and her beguiling voice made her seem magical.

Her makeup was always precise and she wore flowing dresses, with long strings of beads around her neck.

Whereas some of the other young women came down to the kitchen in dressing gowns with their wet hair in turbaned towels, Paula always appeared fully dressed and made up.

Furthermore, her range of clothes seemed endless. She had a different dress on every day, unlike the other women who had a limited number of tops and jeans. Her use of the laundry room was the most frequent in Sue's recollection of any resident past or present.

Yet, Sue thought something didn't ring true about Paula. For such a charismatic and pretty woman she had never given any indication that any men were paying attention to her.

To Sue there was also the curious matter of Paula's insistence on having her own room. Normally women at the refuge were happy to share. Occasionally they might acquire a single room if they were there for a longer stay.

However, Paula had pleaded for one even before she

came. Eventually Sue agreed, thinking that she might have health issues. Surely, it could not just be to accommodate her overflowing wardrobe.

Paula spent a lot of time alone in her room. As Sue passed it one day she heard someone shouting on the phone in a deep, harsh voice.

'Don't ring me again. Damn you! No!'

It sounded like there was a man in her room. She was about to knock to see if she could come to the rescue and to point out that male visitors were not permitted, when the door opened and Paula stepped out. She seemed unaware of Sue and shouted in a gruff voice into her phone as she disconnected, 'Damn you, Germaine!'

Then, noticing that Sue was in the corridor, she instantly recovered her normal mannered voice.

'Why, hello, Sue. I'm afraid I didn't see you there....Err...That's a very nice top you are wearing. I'm just going to make myself some tea. Would you like one?'

'No thanks, I'm going to get myself a strong coffee.'

Paula glided past and Sue followed her downstairs.

At that moment, there was the sound of a young child screaming in the kitchen, and Sue guessed it was the problem child of the new resident.

Paula opened the kitchen door and, as she crossed the room to a young girl in a pushchair, she said calmly, 'Hello, and what's a young lady like you crying about so much?'

Her mother was a woman with short dark hair and shoulder tattoos revealed by a sleeveless black top. She had her back to them and was preoccupied with the kettle on the counter.

'Would you like to play with my beads?' Paula bent down offering the beads still around her neck for the child to touch. She stopped crying immediately.

Her mother turned around and her cross face softened as she saw her daughter engrossed.

'What's your name, then?' Paula asked quietly, smiling at the child's enchanted state.

'Emma,' the girl replied, fingering the beads.

'How did you do that?' asked her mother. 'She's been screaming all day.'

Paula did not answer. She was focussing on playing with the child and maintaining her interest.

It was a fragile peace though. As the mother interrupted further with 'Tell me, how did you do that?' the child started to scream again, but stopped as Paula drew her attention back to the beads.

'Well, you've certainly got some talent there, Paula,' said Sue, watching the now calm child being spoon-fed by her mother.

'Yes, but I can't get more than a few hours work a day at the nursery down the road. I really need to be full-time to get enough money to manage.'

Over the following week, Sue started to consider how she might be able to help.

One afternoon as she was working at her desk, Sue glanced through the basement office window onto the street.

A formidable large woman in her fifties with short cut hair was pacing back and forth on the pavement. It was raining, and the wind was gusting. Her small umbrella repeatedly turned inside out almost as soon as she righted it. She had no protection from the rain, and was getting angrier by the minute.

Finally, she rang the refuge doorbell.

Sue opened the front door and saw the caller's angry face. Water was trickling in several streams down from her soaking wet hair.

'Can you tell Paula I've been waiting out here for over half an hour?'

'Does she know you're coming?'

'I told her I was coming the other day on the phone.'

'And who are you?'

'Germaine, her partner.'

'Her partner?'

'Yes. I've come to take her back. Where is she?'

'Wait here in the hall. I'll see if she's in.'

'I know she is,' asserted Germaine with a scowl as she stepped into the hall and flicked the rain off her umbrella.

Sue went upstairs and knocked on Paula's door.

'Paula, there's someone here to see you.'

'Who is it?' asked Paula from the other side of the door.

'Someone called Germaine.'

'Tell her to go away.'

'You don't want to see her?'

Paula opened the door forcefully. She strode onto the landing and yelled in a deep voice down the stairs. 'Look, I've told you, I'm bloody well not going back to you. Now leave it!'

'Paula,' said Germaine in a condescending voice. 'You can't keep this pretence up any longer. You have to come back with me.'

'No, I don't!' Paula yelled, slamming the door as she strode back into her room.

'Paula, I've told you,' Germaine shouted up the stairs. 'You've no business here. You belong with me.'

Sue was taken aback at the rough tone that Paula had used, but recovered and turned to Germaine to say, 'Well, I'm afraid that's it. She won't see you.'

'Well, he has to, he thinks he'll get enough money by working, but he won't. I can help him, but he'll have to come back.'

'Excuse me, but I'm not following this. You said "he". Who are you talking about? Is it someone Paula knows?'

'Knows?' Germaine gave a low laugh. 'You're dead right in a way, and completely wrong in another. Paula is Paul. Paula is a bloke, or at least he was until a few months ago. He's been saving up for a sex-change operation, but he won't get one on the NHS, I've told him. I could give him the money, but he doesn't want anything to do with me.'

'I don't know about all this,' said Sue, shaking her head in disbelief. 'I think you'd better go for the moment. Just leave me your phone number. I'll have a word with Paula later. This is supposed to be a women-only refuge, so I'll have to think very carefully what to do.'

'Well, make sure you don't take too long. He's unpredictable at times. Very unpredictable. I don't know what he'll do next. He's a real risk to himself.'

Germaine turned, wrenched open the front door, and strode down the street. In her rage, in spite of the torrential rain, she no longer attempted to use her umbrella.

After Sue had allowed time for Paula to calm down, and she herself had spent a quiet hour ordering online groceries, she knocked on Paula's door.

Paula let her in, and then sat on the bed.

'It's rather awkward,' began Sue, her arms folded, as she leant against the closed door. 'Germaine said some strange things. Are they true?'

'I don't want to go back to her.'

'No, but is it true?'

Paula looked down for a moment, then looked up and said, 'Actually I'm on hormone tablets. I was born Paul, a man, but I've always felt that I was a woman. So, I got a referral to a gender reassignment clinic. They put me on a waiting list, but then just recently they said that I'm not suitable. But I am. They suggested I go private, but I haven't got any money. Germaine said that she would fund me if I went and stayed with her. She was in love with me, but I fell out of love with her when she got so possessive. I know this place is for women only, but please let me stay. I've nowhere else, and I need money for another operation.'

'Why on earth did you let Germaine know where you were staying?' Sue asked.

Paula paused and looked down thoughtfully.

'I had to. She insisted... No, the truth is... she was blackmailing me, and she still is. She says that if I don't go back to her she is going to tell the manager at the nursery that I am a man. I'll lose the job that I love, and I'll never be able to save enough money to go to Thailand to have my operation.'

Paula burst into tears and Sue held her hand in an attempt to comfort her but in her heart she knew that what Paula really needed now was practical help.

'Paula, I do understand and sympathise. But technically, although you look and feel like a woman, you are still a man. My managers might have rules about whether they can allow you to stay. I'll speak to them. I'm sorry, but that's all I can do at the moment.'

Sue left, feeling that this situation was totally unsatisfactory. She could only hope that her managers would look kindly on Paula's plight and would not order Sue to tell her to leave.

A week later, and still nothing had filtered down to Sue. It seemed that the managers were waiting to see if there was a problem. This would give them an excuse to solve the situation easily.

Sue was worried over the delay, and feared what might happen if the other residents found out about Paula's biological gender. Some of them were beginning to remark on how emotional Paula was getting, and wondered if anything was stressing her.

Paula had continued to form a relationship with Emma the young child. Weeks ago, her mother had lost her temper several times and had been close to hitting her screaming daughter. However, Emma was a lot calmer whenever Paula spent time playing with her. As Emma's behaviour gradually improved over the ensuing weeks, her mother became more relaxed.

Sue was relieved that mother and child were still together. A foster placement for Emma had certainly been on the cards before Paula had intervened.

Sue admired Paula's talent and ability. Indeed, from feedback at the nursery, where Sue had sensitively enquired, it was clear that she was able to achieve amazing results even with the most difficult of autistic children.

One morning Paula told Sue that she had received a letter from the private gender reassignment clinic in Thailand requesting immediate payment of their fees or they would have to remove her from their list. Paula realised that she would never be able to afford that kind of money and even considered taking an overdose to end her life. She had been troubled by mood swings from the hormone treatment.

Sue was so moved that she contacted her friend Nina

who was a co-trustee of Rula's fund. Rula was the wealthy Polish countess whom they had helped escape from a controlling servant who had imprisoned for her money. With Sue's help, along with Rula's relatives she had been freed, and was living a happy independent life in the city. In gratitude, she had given Sue a cheque for many thousands of pounds to be used to help women in the refuge.

When Nina heard Paula's story, and Sue's idea, she completely agreed that this was a perfect way to use some of that money.

Together they helped Paula book a flight to Thailand.

A grateful Paula handed in her notice to the Nursery where she worked and told Germaine her threats were now pointless.

A week later Sue had an angry phone call from Germaine. She demanded that Sue should order Paula to ring her back. Germaine had ended with the smug remark, 'She'll spend all that money on a useless idea and will come crying back to me.'

However, months later Sue received a letter from Paula saying that the operation had been a complete success. She had settled in Ireland and had found a manager's post in a nursery, helped by a glowing reference from her last employer and by another from Sue who had praised her skilled work with little Emma.

Paula had settled happily as an Irish woman and had just become engaged to a wonderful man. They had put down a deposit on a small cottage.

Paula had struggled and known so much sadness in her life but now, with help from other women, she had been able to make what seemed an impossible dream come true.

Sue was filled with trepidation on her next visit to see Liz in hospital. Had she made any progress? If not, would such a life be worth living?

To her delight, the staff told her there had been a big improvement. She found Liz sitting in a wheelchair in the day room.

'This is mine,' said Liz, beating the arm of her chair. 'I got it today. Do you like it?'

'Yes it's great. I can take you out for a bit of a trip now. Would you like to go down to the hospital tea bar?'

'I don't know,' Liz frowned.

'Well I'll check with the staff. I'm sure it will be OK, and the change will do you good.'

After the nurse had said it was fine for Liz to go off the ward for a cup of tea, Sue helped Liz put her jacket on. It was difficult as Liz was very tense and her arm was stiff.

'We can come back whenever you want,' Sue reassured her.

On hearing this, Liz relaxed and was able to put on her jacket more easily.

The tea bar was crowded and noisy. Sue left Liz at a table while she queued for their drinks.

When Sue returned, Liz looked pale.

'It is a bit crowded in here isn't it?' said Sue.

As she remarked on this a man bumped into the back of Liz's wheelchair just as she was taking a sip of tea, and some of it spilled into her lap.

She cried out and the other people in the café turned to look.

'I've got to go,' she told Sue.

'But you haven't finished your tea. Let's stay a bit longer?'

'No. No. I want to go back.'

Abandoning their barely-touched cups, Sue stood up, unlocked the wheelchair brakes, and pushed Liz back to the familiarity and peace of her side room on the ward.

Tea was waiting for her on a tray and she lifted the yoghurt pot unsteadily. Sue helped her to peel back the top. She watched how she held the pot very tightly in her left hand and manipulated the spoon with her right.

However, after a while Sue noticed that she continued to scrape the pot with the spoon even though it was empty.

'Are you enjoying that?' Sue asked.

Liz looked at her. 'I want to go home.'

'Well it might be better for you to stay here a bit longer until you are properly well. Where do you want to go when you leave?'

'My own home.'

'But you don't want to go back to that same house, do you?'

There was silence as Liz took this in and then her expression changed. Her head fell on her chest and she dropped the yoghurt pot and spoon on the floor. She sobbed uncontrollably.

Betty's Story

It was snowing outside. On days like this, Sue was thankful to be in the warmth of the refuge. But now she had to go to the corner shop. Cath, her deputy who was just leaving at the end of her shift, told Sue they had run out of teabags. She briefly wondered where they had all gone as she had bought a huge box just a couple of days ago. Speculation was a waste of time, she thought. If she didn't want a bad start to tomorrow, with everyone complaining at breakfast, she must brace herself and face the winter weather.

Sue fastened her weatherproof coat and pulled up the hood as she took the lift from her flat down to the ground floor. 'I really ought to use the stairs,' she thought. She had resolved to do this to help with her constant battle to lose 'just half a stone'. But for now, a walk in this weather was quite enough exercise.

As she opened the back door, an icy blast of stinging snow hit her face. It was hard to make out anything through the blizzard.

She battled against the North-easterly towards the local supermarket. It was nearly five, and should have been rush hour, but deep snow had made the roads impassable. All down the street cars had been abandoned, some even on the pavement. When she reached a row of buildings that provided shelter from the wind, it became eerily quiet.

On the pavement ahead, she saw a large mound of what appeared to be cloth but, as she came nearer, she could tell that it was the crumpled figure of someone lying on the pavement at the bottom of the wall. Sue could tell that it was a woman and, as she got closer, she could make out grey hair and a pale sunken face. The woman must have been at least eighty. She was wearing a short thin coat, no hat or gloves, and she was making a whimpering sound.

Sue bent down to speak to her. 'What's the matter, love?'

'I'm trying to get up. But I can't.'

'Did you fall?'

Sue wondered if she should try to help the woman get to her feet, but hesitated. If the woman had a serious injury, then movement could make it worse.

'No, I'm just a bit tired.'

'Where do you live?'

'Well, round and about here, not far. I'm not sure, now. I've got to get some fish for my husband's tea.' She peered up and down the street.

'I'm Sue. What's your name?'

'Betty. Help me up. Do you know where I am?'

Slowly and carefully, Sue helped her to sit up.

'Perhaps I should go up there.' Betty pointed in the direction of a side street.

'Look, come over to my office. We can ring your husband from there.'

'But I've got to get some fish for his tea.'

Sue took the elderly woman's arm, and noticed scratches and bruises on her wrist.

'What happened here?'

'It must have been an accident. It'll only get worse if I don't get any fish.'

'Well you don't want to stay here in the snow.'

Sue thought she would make a gentle attempt at getting Betty on her feet. Surprisingly, a supporting arm was enough for her to manage to stand.

'Can you walk a little way?

'I think so.'

'I can take you to my place and you can rest and warm up a bit. It's not far.'

They walked slowly to the refuge. From time to time Betty stopped and caught her breath while holding Sue's arm.

Once safely inside the refuge, Sue decided to take Betty down in the lift to her basement office, where they would have some privacy. It was warm and quiet there. Sue was able to see Betty more clearly. She was shivering and her coat was soaked with melted snow. Her wet grey hair hung in wisps around her face.

'Let me get that wet coat off you. I've got a dressing gown you can put on.'

As Sue took the elderly woman's coat off, she saw that not only her wrists but also her arms were covered in bruises and scratches.

'Oh dear. What happened?' she asked quietly.

'Jim did it.'

'Jim?'

Betty didn't reply. She just sat with half-closed eyes staring into space.

Sue decided not to press her at this point.

'I'll just go and get us a drink. Do you like hot chocolate?'

Sue came back from the kitchen with two mugs and drew up a chair next to her.

'Where do you live, Betty?'

'Just down the road.'

'If you tell me where you live I can give you a lift back home.'

'I can't go home yet. I've got to get some fish for my husband's tea.'

Betty stood up, spilling some of the hot chocolate on the carpet. She started to pull off the dressing gown as she took a few steps towards the door.

'I've got to go now. I'm in the wrong place. Will I get into trouble?'

'Just wait with me a bit and we'll sort it all out. Sit down and have a rest.' Sue led Betty back to the chair and she slumped into it.

After a few minutes, the warmth of the office fire took effect. Betty relaxed, leaned back in the chair, and soon fell asleep.

'Poor woman,' Sue thought. 'She's so frightened and exhausted.'

Sue was thinking of asking her friend, Police Sergeant Jade, to come around. However, before accusing anyone she wanted to find out more about 'Jim' – whoever he was. Still, she thought she should ring Jade anyway to let the police know what she was going to do.

Sue lifted the telephone and crept out of the room. Standing by the open office door, she dialled Jade's number.

'Hi, Sue, are you snowed in?' Jade's voice came clearly down the line.

'Yes, but it seems to have stopped now,' Sue replied quietly so as not to wake Betty. She briefly peered out of the window. 'Listen, you won't believe this. I found an old lady sitting in the snow and I've brought her back to the refuge.'

'So, you haven't got enough to do already?'

Sue laughed. 'I have, but the poor woman is really confused. Her arms and legs are covered in bruises and she says someone called Jim did it.'

'Where did you find her?'

Sue told her.

'Oh,' said Jade. 'I think I know who your lady is. Her name is Betty Stratton. Her son phoned the station a few hours ago to report her missing. He says she often wanders off. She seems to have travelled a bit further today. She used to live in your area years ago. Once, a gang of youths tried to rob her. Luckily, someone stepped in and stopped it. We've got that on CCTV. It might have happened again. Her son will be so pleased she's safe. I'll give him a ring now and I can take her back.'

'No, it's alright. I can take her if you like. She's used to me now, and anyway the weather's improved.' Sue wanted to explore more of Betty's background, even though her home was across the other side of town.

'Oh, thanks. That's great. She'll be fine when she sees her son.' Jade signed off.

Sue helped Betty into her car and they drove across

town. They pulled up in front of a mid-terraced house, with flaking paint and drawn curtains in the front room.

A short stocky man in his late forties stood at the open front door. He had a shaved head and the stubble of a beard.

'Good Lord, mother! What's happened to you?' His eyebrows raised in concern.

Sue thought he looked angry, but she put it down to the worry of trying to find his mother and fearing for her safety.

Once they were inside the man explained that his father, Jim, had died five years ago. Recently his mother had not been coping and so he had come back to live in the family home to look after her. She had her own bedroom downstairs at the front of the house, and the use of a shared lounge and bathroom at the back. The rest of the house was his domain.

Betty's room was near to the front door so it was quite easy for her to get out. Her son turned the light on while Sue helped Betty into her armchair at the foot of her bed. There were dingy curtains; an old upholstered armchair; and a bedside table on which was a radio, an alarm clock, a rickety lamp and a plastic glass with water in. The drab floral wallpaper badly needed replacing. The ceiling was cobwebbed and grubby. There was a picture of a man in his seventies on the sideboard, presumably Betty's late husband Jim. Sue noted that there was a newly-fitted bolt on the outside of Betty's room.

'Mother, where did you get those bruises?' her son asked, lightly touching her arm.

'No, don't do it. Get off! Get away!' Betty flinched.

'Calm down, Betty,' Sue said. 'You're with friends now. You're back home.'

'She's been missing all afternoon,' he said. 'She must have slipped the front door latch whilst I wasn't looking. The police told me that they thought she had been attacked by a gang again. But she's home now. I can take care of her. Thanks very much for bringing her back. I'll get these injuries checked by a nurse at the local surgery.'

After leaving, Sue felt uneasy about what she had seen, but realised that Betty might well be confused about how she had come by her injuries.

The next day Sue shared her concerns with Jade over the

phone, but Jade told her that the police felt the situation had been resolved.

However, Sue was not totally reassured by this. Back in the office, she had an idea. Maybe the police hadn't got all the up to date information. She asked her technical expert friend Nina to check for any street cameras that might shed light on Betty's wanderings.

A couple of hours later Nina rang back to say that she had located an image of a woman matching Betty's description struggling through the snow along the streets at about the right time.

'There are a few minutes where she meets a gang of youths. They run around and poke fun. One of them pulls at her coat, but they do not hit her. This is late in her walk. The bruises might already be on her.'

A few days later Sue was disturbed to find Betty wandering in a street near to the refuge yet again. She took her straight home.

Betty's son met them at the front door, and she flinched as he led her by the arm into her shabby room.

With Betty safely settled in her armchair, Sue closed the door and spoke to the son quietly in the back room.

The back room where he lived had freshly painted walls, and contained a state-of-the-art home cinema with large curved plasma TV and surround-sound speakers. There were expensive wall lights, a luxurious white leather suite and a designer glass coffee table. The sideboard hosted a wide assortment of malt whisky bottles.

He confided in Sue that his father, Jim, used to beat his mother up when he was younger, and that both his parents had been strict with him.

When Sue suggested that she could call again, he told her not to bother. They didn't need carers because he was out of work with a bad back, and was at home a lot of the time. It was just unfortunate that Betty had been able to slip out a couple of times without his seeing.

He added he had no idea how she got her injuries. 'There are plenty of bad people on the streets. They could easily mug her. She is very vulnerable. But fortunately the nurse I took her to see at the clinic says her injuries are not serious.'

That evening when Sue was on duty at the refuge, she spoke to her deputy Cath about the visit and her continuing unease about Betty's situation.

'Strange that you should mention it,' Cath said. 'One of the residents knows that street. She was telling me about a bloke who lives along there who nearly killed his girlfriend because she was going to leave him. In the end, she managed to get away and didn't press charges. I'm wondering if it's the same bloke?'

Sue shuddered as it brought back memories of the terrible attack on Liz.

The next day Sue still couldn't get these thoughts out of her mind. She mentioned it to Jade who checked the police database, and told her that no one at Betty's address had a police record.

Sue was still not satisfied and asked Nina for advice about the best way to find out who had injured Betty.

Nina said, 'If you think it's the son, then I can let you have a micro camera. What is the furniture like in there?'

'There was a big upholstered armchair.'

'With buttons? What kind? Can you remember?'

'Well yes, ordinary. Nothing special. Just normal black vinyl if I remember right.'

'Excellent. I have got a micro spy camera disguised as a button that might do. It is a Russian model and, as you say in English, high spec. If you can find an excuse to get in there again, then you might be able to install it if he is not looking. Come around tomorrow.'

The next day Sue collected the camera from Nina. It was just like a normal upholstery nail with a longer shaft that served as an antenna.

Sue was thinking of an excuse to visit. However, as there were no further instances of Betty being found on the street, she took a chance, and drove around to call unprompted.

Sue knocked at the front door but there was no answer. Instinctively she tried the handle. The door opened.

She shouted hello, but there was no reply. She stepped inside.

Sue could not believe her luck as she went into Betty's

room and found her in bed and asleep.

As quietly as she could, Sue flipped out one of the upholstery buttons with the aid of a penknife, and inserted the camera button in its place. It looked almost identical and, as the armchair was at the foot of the bed, its wide-angle lens would be able to film what went on in the area around the bed.

Suddenly there was noise from the room above and footsteps on the stairs. Betty's son appeared, bleary-eyed, and smelling of whisky. He demanded to know what Sue was doing there.

Sue held her ground. 'I just popped in on the off-chance to see how your mother is.'

'Get out!' he shouted, raising his fist.

Sue realised she had no grounds for being there and had better make a swift exit.

'I only called as a friend to see how Betty was getting on,' she shouted back to him as she drove off in her car.

Once around the corner she pulled in to phone Nina and tell her that she had planted the tiny camera.

'I know,' said Nina. 'I am getting a good signal from it. Well done. I will monitor it for this evening and the whole of tomorrow. I will let you know if we pick up anything incriminating.'

The next evening, around seven, Sue's office phone rang. It was Nina.

'You should see this recording,' she said. 'It looks bad. Most of the day Betty is locked in her room. You can see her trying to get out and she seems to be shouting for help. Yesterday evening the son comes in to get her ready for bed. She wants to go upstairs, but he gets angry, pulls her back, and throws her onto the bed. He locks the door. In the late morning today he brings her a cup of tea and a slice of bread. He dresses her on the commode. Then he locks her in her room and only returns at lunchtime with chips in a box.'

'Phone an ambulance to meet me at Betty's house,' said Sue decisively. 'I'm going there right now.'

She drove around as fast as she could to Betty's home.

She managed to talk her way in by saying that she was paying Betty a quick visit on her way home. Her son smelled of whisky, but he was reasonably well-mannered this time.

Then Sue dropped her bombshell.

'We know who's been hurting Betty, and we've got the evidence. An ambulance is on its way.'

He was silent, the colour rose in his cheeks and he looked down to avoid Sue's gaze.

The ambulance crew appeared a few minutes later. They had no difficulty taking Betty past the seemingly mystified son and into the ambulance.

'It's OK,' Sue told the ambulance crew. 'I'll speak to her son. I'm from Social Services.'

After the ambulance had taken Betty, Sue said, 'Betty wasn't confused at all about who was hitting her, was she?'

The son blustered. 'She was just remembering what my Dad, Jim, did to her. Living in the past.'

'No. She knows what's happening. It was you who hit her. You're Jim too, aren't you? The same name as your father? And we know that you beat up other women as well.'

'How dare you bring that up? How did you know?'

'I have contacts.'

'They're liars!'

'The ambulance crew saw your mother had fresh bruises.'

'You don't know how difficult she can be. Especially to me, her own son.'

'An abuser always says they were provoked. That is no excuse at all.'

'Something seemed to take me over once I had the drink. She wouldn't just get into bed and go to sleep. She wouldn't leave me in peace.' His face reddened. 'I didn't know what I was doing.'

'Maybe you were copying your dad, beating up a woman for any slight reason.'

'She was bad to me when I was young. She split me up from my first girlfriend. I've never forgiven her.'

'So that's why you resent your mother, and wallop her for any slight thing she does?'

'You don't know her,' Jim said. 'Now she's gone senile, my life is a misery. Perhaps it is all too much and she should go into residential care. I've reached the end of my tether. You are right. She'd be better off in a home.'

'Oh no, I don't think so. It's her house. You can't throw her out. But legally she can throw <u>you</u> out.'

Betty stayed in hospital for a few days and improved with treatment for malnutrition. She came home with carers who would call frequently. Sue was at the house to welcome her as Jim was packing up his belongings to go and stay with his brother.

'Perhaps she might let you visit her when things have calmed down,' said Sue. 'But that is for her to say. For the moment you had better stay away.'

Back at the refuge, Sue updated Nina over the phone.

'Good job he does not know how we got the evidence, so do not tell him,' Nina said. 'What we have done is illegal, but necessary. I think we will keep all this on file, and keep the camera active.'

'We've no need to tell the carers,' Sue added. 'Who knows, we might need more evidence one day. He's very plausible and it could happen again in the future, but somehow I don't think it will. We'll be keeping an eye on him. If only we had been able to do that with Viktor, it might have saved Liz.'

A few days later Sue visited Liz at the hospital. The doors to the neurorehabilitation unit opened automatically as Sue approached. Earlier in the week, when she had made her usual phone call to the ward, she had been told that Liz was going to be transferred here. The light, airy space of the new unit contrasted favourably with the hot and stuffy atmosphere of the medical ward.

A cluster of patients sat watching television in the day room. Sue couldn't see Liz so she passed through and down a corridor to an open plan physiotherapy area, lined with handrails. There were examination couches, a set of practice stairs, a large orange ball, and stacked weights. A physiotherapist was assisting a patient walking while holding onto parallel rails, but both were so focussed on the task they didn't notice Sue.

As she didn't want to interrupt, she continued down the corridor to a door labelled Occupational Therapy. She looked through the glass window in the door and saw Liz at a table with a therapist who was wearing white top and green trousers. As she tapped on the glass window the therapist looked up, and Liz turned and smiled in recognition. The therapist gestured for her to come in.

'Hello, I'm Sue Barlow, Liz's friend.'

'Oh, pleased to meet you. Liz has told me all about you. Please take a seat.'

'You're looking well,' Sue greeted Liz.

'Yes,' the therapist agreed. 'She's made great progress in just the few days she's been with us.'

'I have,' Liz acknowledged. 'But I'm still dwelling on what happened. I can't wait to put it behind me and move on.'

'That's great, but you must take it steady.' Sue replied.

'I expect I'll be out very soon.'

'In time,' said the therapist. 'But you will need to be here for around a month. You can walk a few steps with one person, but you need a wheelchair for longer distances.'

'I'm going on a home visit soon. I can't wait. This is going to be the start of my new life.'

Viv's Story

'Get over here. Now!'
Viv's angry shout to her son in the hallway carried down to Sue's basement office. She knew it was time to tackle Viv about the way she was treating Jamie. Poor kid, he was only four and was a quiet, almost withdrawn, child.

Viv had been at the refuge for over a week. She had left Steve, her husband, because she said he hit her all the time. She told Sue that she had caught him recently giving Jamie slaps around the head, and that was the last straw.

Viv would shout and scream at Jamie over the slightest thing, losing her temper with him for making any noise. He only did what most four-year-olds do. Like picking toys up and dropping them to see what happened or kicking a ball around the room. Sometimes he would bang things together very loudly. Any noise he made angered Viv.

Until now the other women in the refuge had been too frightened to say anything to Viv directly, but recently a few of them had come to tell Sue that they were concerned.

Sue didn't normally like to intervene because she knew women in Viv's situation were going through so much stress. Usually things settled down in time. But this was different.

Sue got up from her desk and walked up the stairs to the hallway.

'Why are you so angry with Jamie?' she asked Viv.

Viv glared, 'He's my kid. It's none of your business.'

She turned to Jamie who was trying to crash two small toy cars together on the floor. 'Stop that!' she barked.

Sue tried to calm her. 'I know how upset you are. I only want to help. Would you like to talk about it? I can ask someone to look after Jamie for a while.'

'No thanks – I'm off out,' Viv answered abruptly and, grabbing Jamie by the hand, she rushed back to her room.

That evening at supper Viv's mood had changed completely. She looked relaxed, joking and laughing with the other residents. When she saw Sue, she came over and said quietly, 'I'm really sorry for how I spoke to you this morning. You were only trying to help. I just lose it sometimes. Jamie is a difficult kid. He knows how to wind me up.'

'Look, Viv, I guess you are going to have to stay here for a bit while you get things sorted. How about next week I ask someone from the Children's Centre to come around and work with Jamie?'

'OK, I'll give it a go,' Viv agreed.

Sue felt a good deal happier when she heard this.

Certainly, over the next few days, Viv seemed to calm down and stopped shouting and criticising Jamie.

However, the following Sunday morning Sue heard Viv shouting again. Although it was raining, she rushed out with Jamie in her usual state of embattlement. 'You want to go to the bloody park,' she yelled. 'Well, just see how you like it getting soaked in this rain.' She strode out, dragging Jamie with her.

Shortly afterwards all the other mums with kids had gone out too, and the refuge was unusually quiet. Sue thought she would take advantage of this and plough through some of the ever-growing pile of paper work. It was not her idea of a great way to spend a Sunday, but it had to be done.

Cath, her deputy, had come in for a couple of hours to

help sort out the case records that head office was insisting should include more detail. Cath had previously worked in a prison, and was good at record-keeping, but sometimes her critical attitude towards residents was hard for Sue to cope with.

Cath looked up from one of the case notes and remarked, 'This is the seventh one we've found with the man's date of birth missing. I reckon it's been left off on purpose. These women still try to protect the bloke. You think they would know better. It's their own fault it keeps happening to them.'

Sue opened her mouth to correct her, but she was interrupted by a loud shout from the front hall above her basement office.

Viv had come bursting back into the refuge after just twenty minutes, leaving the front door open in the stormy weather.

She screamed, 'He's gone! He's gone!'

Sue came up to the hall and caught hold of the wild-eyed Viv.

'Who's gone?'

'My Jamie! He's been taken!'

'Who's taken him? What happened?'

'It was Steve, my ex. I saw him. He came out of nowhere. He snatched Jamie off the swings and ran off with him into a van. He had somebody with him driving. It's kidnap! Phone the police! Phone the police!'

'Calm down, Viv. I'll phone the police. Just come and sit here in the office.'

Cath gestured to a spare chair by the desk, but Viv would not sit down.

Sue phoned Jade and gave her Viv's description of Steve and the van.

Viv hovered in an agitated state, trying to overhear the phone conversation.

'Where could he have taken him?' Sue asked Viv, with Jade still on the line.

'I don't know. Maybe his flat?'

'Where's that?'

'I don't know. He's moved. Somewhere up the north side I think, by Olympus Street.'

Sue relayed this to Jade, who suggested that Viv should ring Steve's mobile.

Cath shuffled her papers and tried to ignore the drama.

Viv held Sue's phone to her ear, paused for Steve to answer, and shouted into it.

'You bastard! Don't you hurt him! You bastard! I'll kill you for this!'

'Let me talk to him,' said Sue, reaching for the phone.

'You bastard!' Viv ranted. 'I've got Social Services here and the police are on their way. They'll be shutting you away for a long time. Here's my social worker. She'll tell you!'

Viv thrust the phone at Sue.

Sue collected her thoughts. 'Hello, is that Steve? It's Sue here from the refuge. Don't worry. I only want to help. We can talk this through, Steve.'

'What?' Viv shouted. 'Talk it through? No way.' She grabbed the phone, tilting it towards her while it was still in Sue's grasp. 'I'm going to get you for this! You evil bastard!'

Cath raised her eyes to the ceiling as Sue calmly tilted the phone back towards her own ear, saying, 'Steve, we can work this out. Now, is Jamie safe?'

'Yeah," Sue heard Steve say. "No thanks to Viv. Can I come round to explain?'

'No. We can't tell you the address of the refuge. You'll have to keep on having access somewhere else, under supervision. That's what the court has ruled. Now tell me where you are. Otherwise, you're only making it harder for yourself and Jamie.'

'I'm not giving him up.'

'You know you can't snatch the child like that. It's a breach of the court order, but we can discuss it. Where are you now?'

Sue got the address and rang it through to Jade who agreed to meet her there.

Viv overheard Sue giving the address.

'That's his parents'!' Viv exclaimed. 'Come on, let's go.'

'It's best if you stay with Cath for now.' Sue pointed at the empty chair next to where Cath was sitting. 'I can get it sorted quicker that way,' said Sue reaching for her coat and bag.

Persuaded by Cath and Sue, Viv eventually sat down.

As Sue drove around to Steve's parents she thought that Viv, in her present state, might lose control and then the police would have to be formally involved. In that context there would be no doubt that Steve, who did not have custody, had effectively kidnapped his son.

Sue was concerned. She knew of men who had harmed, even killed, their own children to get back at the woman who had split the family apart.

Outside the house, she parked up behind Jade's car. The two women walked up the garden path and pressed the doorbell of a well-kept semi-detached house. They were surprised at the appearance of the young man who opened the door. He was about thirty, slightly built and wearing glasses. He did not in any way fit the picture of the physically abusive character that Viv had painted. But, as Sue reflected, there was no way of predicting who would be violent from how they looked. When Sue and Jade had explained who they were, they were surprised yet again when he invited them inside without the slightest hesitation.

As they entered the warm, well-furnished living room they saw Jamie sitting on the couch between a man and woman in their sixties. The woman was reading to Jamie. Sue immediately saw a difference in the child. He stretched contentedly across the woman's lap to see the pictures in the book she was holding. As she read to him, his face lit up with a smile. The first smile Sue had ever seen him give.

Steve introduced his parents, Joan and Brian.

'You know Jamie should really be with his mother because she's got custody,' Jade pointed out to Steve. 'I'm not here in an official capacity today, but I hope we can sort things out without formal police involvement. I think Viv will be OK about your bringing him here because we can see he's being well cared for.'

'A lot better than she ever did,' Joan muttered as Jamie cuddled up closer to her.

'Mum...don't!' Steve pleaded.

'Just tell them why you brought Jamie back here from

the park,' said Joan.

Sue and Jade looked enquiringly at Steve.

'I didn't mean to,' Steve said. 'I just wanted to make sure he was safe. I'd found which area the refuge was in and I got a friend to drive me there. I was watching today because I guessed Viv would want to go out. I followed her to the park. She just let Jamie run off to the swings on his own. Then she got the bottle out of her bag. Same as usual... a water bottle full of vodka and orange squash. She thinks people won't know what it is. She was drunk and completely out of it. Anyone could have taken Jamie. It's only because he shouted, 'It's Daddy!' that she noticed me. I didn't stop to think. I just picked him up and ran. My mate drove us home. Then I phoned Mum and Dad. I knew Viv would soon get someone to come round.'

Joan added that Viv had been a drinker for years, and that Steve only stayed with her for Jamie's sake. 'He never hit her like she said in the custody case, and he certainly would never touch Jamie. Jamie is his world.'

'I didn't hit Viv, but I did try to hold her back when she was trying to hurt Jamie,' Steve admitted. 'Then she fell and sprained her wrist. She took herself off to accident and emergency. Of course, she had a load of other bruises she could show them – from falling over drunk. But she said it was me who hit her. Worst of all, she told them that I was doing it to Jamie. It was all lies.'

Although Sue was usually sympathetic to women's ill treatment, she began to be persuaded by Steve's emotional version of how he had been wrongly accused.

'I'm really sorry, Steve, but until the court can sort everything out, we have to take Jamie back to the refuge. But I promise we'll be watching out to make sure he's safe. From now on we'll be keeping a note of how Viv behaves with him.'

Jade and Sue rose to leave and had a hard time persuading Jamie to come with them. He clung to his father in a desperate attempt to stay with him. It was heartbreaking.

On their way back to the refuge, Jamie cried himself to sleep in the car.

Viv was waiting for them in the lounge, and when she saw Jamie she made a big show of their reunion. She cried and held him tight, but Sue noted the child's frozen expression and how he tried to draw away from his mother.

'I suppose Steve told you a pack of lies about why he took Jamie,' Viv said. 'He can be very convincing when he wants to be. You don't know him like I do. Are they going to prosecute him for kidnapping, then?'

'I can't really say at the moment,' Jade replied.

'Anyway, it's all sorted for the moment, thank goodness,' Sue said.

Just then Jade's mobile rang and she turned away from them to answer it. 'Tell the store detective I'm on my way.'

'Sorry I've got to go on another case,' she said, moving to the door.

After Jade had left, Viv took Jamie up to her room. Sue went down to her office, intending to carry on with the paperwork. However, her deputy Cath had gone off duty, so Sue gave up on the case notes and made herself a much-needed cup of tea.

A little later she peeped around the door of the residents' lounge. She saw Jamie sitting among a pile of toys. He was alone and still, and showed no interest in playing with them. Viv was on the other side of the room reading a magazine, and taking a drink from what looked like a bottle of orange juice.

A few days later Viv told Sue that she had decided to go back to live with Steve at his flat. She wanted to give him another chance. He had pushed her around, but she thought a lot of it was caused by the stress of dealing with his interfering parents. Sue was pleased that Steve could be with his son but, just the same, she knew the situation was far from ideal. She asked the area Social Services Team and the Health Visitors to make early follow-up visits.

However, within a couple of days Viv had readmitted herself to the refuge as an emergency. She had come via the local hospital accident and emergency again. This time it was Jamie who had been injured. He had cigarette burns on his hands and his back and he would not say who had done it. In fact, he hardly spoke at all now. Sue was shocked when she saw him. He looked thin, pale and uncared for. His clothes were grubby, and his hair obviously had not been washed since he had left the refuge.

'Hello Jamie. It's lovely to see you. Would you like a biscuit? I've got some of those pink wafer ones you like.'

Jamie did not answer. He just stared blankly at Sue.

Sue asked Cath to take Jamie to have a wash and change of clothes while she sat down to talk to Viv.

Viv told Sue how things had started off well at home, as she had put her foot down about Steve's parents coming around almost every five minutes. Then one day she had asked Steve for some money for groceries.

'He went mad. He grabbed Jamie and shook him in front of me and then he lit a cigarette and burned him where you can see. He's a monster. I'll never go back to him.'

Sue listened and again was swayed by Viv's account of things, but she resolved to follow her instincts and to observe her carefully while she was in the refuge.

One day, soon afterwards, Sue was in the kitchen when Viv came in to cook some food and she had a face like thunder.

'What's the matter?' asked Sue.

'There are problems with the bank account. Payment delays. Money that I was expecting from Steve has gone into the wrong account because he got my bank details wrong. So, I'm a good few quid short this week. I'm fed up with it! The bank won't play ball and they say it's my fault. It's going to take ages to sort out.'

'Hang on a minute. Calm down.'

Viv didn't. She stormed off to her room with a bowl of cereal for Jamie. Sue followed her, but Viv slammed the door behind her.

Outside the room, Sue could hear Viv shouting angrily at Jamie. 'What's this? Why aren't you dressed? What's this mess here?'

'No, Mommy, no! Don't hit me.'

There was a slap and Jamie burst out crying.

'You do that again and you'll be for it!'

Sue paused outside the door, aware that it was against refuge policy to go into someone's room without permission. But when she heard slap after slap, and scream after scream, she knew she must go into that room and face Viv's anger before Jamie was harmed.

Sue thrust open the door. The first thing she saw was Jamie cowering in a corner with Viv towering over him holding an empty bottle in a raised hand.

When Viv saw Sue, her anger knew no bounds. 'Get out, bitch!' she screamed, and threw the bottle.

Sue instinctively put her hand up to her eyes to shield them.

The bottle smashed against the wall, narrowly missing Sue's shoulder. It shattered, sending shards of glass flying around the room.

Viv picked up another bottle.

Then there was a shout from behind Sue.

'Put that bottle down!'

It came from Cath, who was on duty. Fortunately for Sue, Cath had experience of defusing crisis situations from her previous work in a prison. She easily disarmed Viv and pushed her down into a chair.

Sue scooped Jamie up into her arms.

After the police were called and Viv had been taken away, Sue and Cath looked around Viv's room. Every drawer and cupboard were full of empty bottles and some unopened ones containing cheap vodka. It was clear that Viv was a long-standing aggressive alcoholic. She had lied about Steve, but perhaps in her mind she thought it was the truth.

A social worker came to see if Jamie should be taken into a foster home for a while. However, Sue convinced her that Steve's parents would be the best people to care for him until the inevitable future custody hearing.

Sue took Jamie in her car to Steve's parents' home, and tears came to her eyes when she saw Jamie run to be hugged by his Grandma and Grandad.

Later Steve told Sue that an enraged Viv had burned

Jamie with cigarettes when Steve refused to give her money to buy more drink. However the police had believed Viv's story that Steve was the abuser.

Some months later, there was a custody hearing at the Family Court. Based on Sue's evidence, the original decision was reversed and Steve obtained full custody of his son.

Viv was allowed supervised access but she never attended, and nothing more was heard of her.

The next time Sue visited Liz she found her sitting in her room by her bed.

Her children, Heather and Toby were there too. Toby was wheeling a little toy train around the floor. Heather was sitting on the bed showing Liz books where she had done her schoolwork.

Sue told Liz about Viv and how her little boy was now safe and happy with his father and grandparents.

'We don't know where Viv is now. She disappeared without leaving any message. She could be anywhere.'

Liz wondered how on earth Viv could have taken off and left her child behind. She looked fondly at her own children and Sue knew they meant everything to her.

Liz said how grateful she was to her parents, Trish and Andy, for looking after the children and for offering to let her sleep in a downstairs room. Her children, Heather and Toby, had the remaining two bedrooms upstairs.

'I had a great home visit yesterday,' she told Sue. 'They said that at this rate I'll soon be going home for good.'

Ebele's Story

From a darkened room police sergeant Jade Norton looked through the one-way screen into a brightly-lit interview room in the airport operations centre. It was bare and painted white with just a table and two chairs. A customs officer sat on one of the chairs. Opposite her was a woman with a little girl of about four on her lap. Jade had been told by the customs officials that these people were Nigerian.

There was an open suitcase on the table between the woman and the customs officer. A large amount of cash in fifty-pound notes was lying on top of the clothes.

'Thirty thousand pounds is a lot of money to take with you if you're just going on a short holiday, Ebele,' Jade heard the customs officer say as he peered over his glasses.

He pointed to the suitcase and studied Ebele's face for any reaction. There was not the slightest flicker of emotion.

Jade got out her mobile and walked to a corner of the room away from the glass screen. She dialled Sue.

'Hi Sue,' she whispered. 'I'd be really grateful for your help. I'm trying to find some information about a lady who says she is going to Nigeria to visit her mother for a few weeks. But, we can't let her go with the amount of money she wants to take out the country. She says she is a pharmacist. I'm sure something's up. It looks as if she is running scared and she won't talk about it. Maybe she needs a night or two at the refuge?'

'We might have a bed. What's her name?'

'Ebele Bantu. I'm trying to get some info on her but the connection is poor. I've a feeling there's something wrong with her story and, quite honestly, I'm worried about the little girl she has with her. I'm guessing it's her daughter, but I do need to check it out.'

'OK, no problem,' said Sue. 'Just let me know their address and dates of birth. I'll ask Nina. She can get information that you probably won't be able to access easily. Just don't ask how.'

'I'm certainly not going to ask questions,' said Jade. 'And anyway, I'm no expert. I know that your Russian friend is, though. Thanks so much.'

Jade went into the interview room and sat down next to the customs officer opposite Ebele.

'Please can I go now?' said Ebele. 'My flight is in an hour. If I miss it, I don't know what I'll do.'

'If you tell us the truth you might be able to make it,' said Jade. 'But I'm not convinced you are just flying out to see your mother.'

'I am.'

'Look. We can sit here all day and night with me asking questions and you telling lies, but that's not right for your little girl. I'm thinking now about calling Social Services to take her to foster parents for the time being.'

Ebele nodded her head and looked relieved. Jade was amazed that, instead of the expected shock and protest, Ebele seemed to welcome this suggestion.

Jade left the room to speak with the customs officers in private, to see if they had any more information she could use. While she was talking to them, and drinking a welcome cup of coffee, her mobile rang.

'Hi, it's Sue. I've just phoned Nina and found some information about your lady. Everything seems to be in order. She does work as a pharmacist and is taking some extended annual leave to visit Nigeria for a holiday. The little girl is her daughter, and her name is Felicia. She goes to nursery school and there aren't any concerns about her. In fact, they think she is a very bright child. There is another person living at Ebele's address though. He has only been there for three months. His name is John Adewumi.'

'Great. Thanks, Sue. I owe you one.'

Jade walked back into the interview room. Ebele seemed a little more relaxed. Someone had brought juice and biscuits and Ebele was encouraging Felicia to eat.

'Does John know you are taking so much money away with you?'

This time Ebele did react. She raised her head and met Jade's gaze. There was raw fear in her eyes as she instinctively drew her daughter closer.

'Have you been talking to him? Does he know where we are? If he does, then no one is safe.'

'What do you mean?' Jade asked. 'If he is dangerous we can protect you. Just trust me and tell me what is happening.'

Ebele looked at her daughter for some time and finally spoke in a broken voice. 'A friend asked us to put him up three months ago. He behaved well at the beginning but then he had a phone call from Nigeria and he changed. He wouldn't let us go out of the house, and he was always so angry with Felicia. Then I learned the truth. He is a witch-hunter. He thinks this lovely little girl, my daughter, is a witch. He has had instructions from the leaders of his sect to kill her. We escaped, but he'll stop at nothing. He always carries a large ceremonial knife and thinks that it has magic in it.'

Felicia squirmed on her mother's lap and said, 'I need the toilet, Mummy.'

Jade nodded to Ebele, 'OK. But make it quick, please. A member of staff will go with you.'

Meanwhile, in her darkened flat, Nina studied her computer screens. After the phone call from Sue, she had tapped into the security surveillance system at the airport. She was interested in seeing the passengers and imagining their stories. There was a frail elderly woman, sitting hunched on a seat surrounded by luggage; a teenager cross-legged on the floor eating a burger with one hand, waving it around as he held an animated conversation on his mobile; and a mournful young man with long dark hair who had the look of a neglected poet. There were numerous security personnel. Not only the obvious armed police, but also probably plain-clothes operatives who could be anyone in the crowd.

Nina reflected on how things are not always what they seem. When she had arrived at this same airport from Russia, she had been asked to speak to customs officers in an interview room. She had travelled wearing a black veil covering all her face except her eyes. Nina guessed the officials thought she was Muslim, but something in her manner had made them suspicious. In the privacy of the small room, she had removed her veil. The customs officer had averted his gaze in horror, and left the room. When he returned he was accompanied by a female social worker.

As they listened to Nina's ordeal of living with Viktor, culminating in the acid attack, they promised to do all they could to help her build a new life. They only saw a victim. They did not realise that Nina was in fact also a hunter determined to track down Viktor and bring other men like him to justice.

She was jolted out of her reverie by the sound of her doorbell. Three short rings. This was the signal she had arranged with Sue.

Nina spent most of her life in this darkened room, not even going out of the building to buy food. She had it all delivered and paid by credit card over the phone. The shop left takeaway meals in the lobby where she would go and collect it after the deliveryman had left.

Nina did not wear a veil as she opened the door to her flat. The two women were more at ease in each other's company now. Sue embraced Nina and handed her a bottle of wine.

'It's just a little thank you for all your help with the hidden camera at Betty's,' Sue said. 'Betty is doing great at home now. Carers come round to help her get up and go to bed. They take her out and make sure she's eating. I think not having enough food and being so frightened was the reason she got confused. She has the whole house to herself now her son, Jim, has moved out. She's really happy. I go to see her regularly. She might want to see Jim again in time, but I'll make sure someone is with her if that happens.'

'That's great news. Come on through. Let's open the wine.'

Sue didn't usually drink in the daytime, but she thought she would do something different today. She had the afternoon off work and it would be good to spend time with Nina, who was such a knowledgeable and interesting friend.

Sue followed Nina to the kitchen where Nina poured two glasses of wine.

'Come through, Sue. I have just been watching the airport departure lounge.'

Sue followed Nina into the darkened room dominated by banks of computer monitors. She sat next to Nina and watched the screen showing the airport lounge.

'This is terrible,' Nina told Sue. 'I have tapped into the police communication system. I overheard a message from Jade to the police station. I will find out some more about this witch-hunter guy, John Adewumi. The young girl is in danger. This is more so now they have left the customs suite even though they have a member of staff with them.'

She turned her back to the airport screen and typed into another computer to do a search.

After about ten minutes watching the airport lounge, Sue's attention was drawn to a large man dressed in a robe that she guessed was traditional African clothing. He had just emerged from the toilets and appeared to be looking for someone. He was pacing up and down in an agitated manner. It seemed that he had something, perhaps a large stick, tucked into the front of his robe against his chest. She couldn't make out exactly what it was. From time to time the man clutched his chest to feel or to steady the object inside his clothing.

'Come and have a look at this,' Sue called out to Nina.

Nina quickly turned to look at Sue's screen. 'God! It is him!'

'Who?'

'John Adewumi, the witch hunter. And we are not the only ones interested in him. There is a security alert on at the airport. See the police taking up their positions?'

On the food court above the departure lounge, half a

dozen police were spaced at regular intervals, some with their guns pointed in Adewumi's direction.

'And see there.' Nina pointed to the frail, bent elderly woman surrounded by luggage. She had straightened up and put her hand inside her coat pocket. 'I thought so. She is plain-clothes security. She has a small firearm in that pocket.'

'What will they do?'

'It all depends how he behaves. That object under his clothes does not look like a gun, but they cannot be sure. If he reaches for it, the marksmen will take him out.'

'You mean they'll shoot and kill him?'

'Yes. And in this case, it might not be such a bad thing. I have looked into his background and chatted with my contacts. He is wanted for murder in Nigeria. He is in a cult that profits by denouncing witches in remote areas. He chooses elderly women or innocent children. He is responsible for having killed and dismembered a child of six. That is probably the tip of the iceberg. In a chat room he claims to have done away with many witches. He says he has dragged their evil souls to God to face judgement.'

Sue looked at Nina. Her face showed a steely determination. Sue had seen this look once before, and that was when Viktor's name had been mentioned.

'I must let Jade know what is happening and how dangerous this guy is. Perhaps it would not be a loss to the world if he was eliminated.' Nina took a long swallow of the wine.

As Nina and Sue stared intently at the monitors, they saw Ebele and Felicia come out of the toilet. In an instant, the man in the robe ran up to them, snatched the child and disappeared into the crowd. They lost sight of him temporarily, but then their attention was drawn to a group of police officers running to surround the entrance of a chemist's store.

Ebele tried to go after Felicia into the chemist's, but she was held back by Jade and several officers at the entrance carrying guns. The shoppers gave them a wide berth. Sue and Nina recognised Adewumi clutching Felicia tightly to his side and pretending to peruse hair products. Each time he moved into another aisle, a police officer moved accordingly to keep him in view through the window, but stopped short of stepping into the store.

Sue and Nina heard Jade reporting to her inspector through the police communication system. 'It's Ebele's daughter, not his. He's apparently been hunting them through London. They're trying to escape from him by going back to Nigeria. He can't follow them there because of warrants out for his arrest. Ebele says he's carrying a large ceremonial knife, and that he's got instructions from his sect leaders to kill Felicia. We don't want to create an incident, but we might have to evacuate the airport.'

'What about interpreters and liaison?" asked Jade's inspector.

'We've asked for local Nigerian-speaking negotiators,' replied Jade. 'But the last one we used was useless and he's not answering his phone. The others will take a few hours to get here. We can't wait that long. We can't stand down, and we can't rush him because we might endanger the child.'

As two of the police officers took a step inside the store, Adewumi tightened his grasp on Felicia and shouted, 'Don't come near! I'll kill the child and everyone!'

Sue watched as Nina brought a microphone to her mouth and clicked Jade's number on her screen. Jade answered, and Nina said, 'Give me Adewumi's number. I know his dialect and I can negotiate for you.'

Realising this would be an unorthodox procedure, Jade hesitated. Then she decided that, although far from ideal, this distance negotiation was worth a try given there were so few remaining options. After a moment's hesitation, she asked Ebele to give her Adewumi's mobile number.

Nina opened a translation programme and clicked on the dialect of Adewumi's Nigerian home district. She dialled his mobile, and patched Jade in. Though Jade could hear the conversation, it was in another language and meant nothing to her.

'I have an important message for you,' Nina said. 'I am speaking on behalf of the elders in your home district. You have done well to hunt the witch down. Now all will work out in your favour and you will be honoured and rewarded. Do you have a gun?'

'No, but I have a powerful weapon that will kill the witch and the demons that are protecting her,' Adewumi replied in his native language.

'You know the demons are all around you,' said Nina. 'They are attracted to the child. They will be distracted and mean you no harm if you put the child down.'

Slowly he let Felicia go. She ran towards the door where one of the police officers stepped forward and grabbed her. The other drew a Taser.

'Now,' Nina said, 'while the demons are not looking, you can kill them all with your weapon.'

Adewumi started to pull the knife from under his robe and pointed it at the police officer who had stepped forward to recover the child. As soon as he did so, the other police officer shot him with the Taser.

Adewumi dropped to the floor in a spasm.

As Sue and Nina continued to watch the CCTV, they saw Adewumi being handcuffed, hauled to his feet, and led away. Ebele and Felicia were reunited, shedding tears of joy and relief.

'Maybe it was not exactly fair to trap him like that,' laughed Nina.

'But it worked well,' said Sue, laughing too.

Ebele was given a reward by the Nigerian government for helping with the arrest. Later Sue learned that the Nigerian police were also able to track down the rest of the gang after questioning Adewumi. They were now all in a Nigerian prison awaiting trial.

Sue rang the bell of a small semi in a quiet cul-de-sac. The house was bordered by a well-trimmed privet hedge, and had a short narrow driveway with space for one car.

She waited for some time, and then heard sounds from inside of someone slowly coming to the front door. Finally, Liz opened it. She was wearing a tracksuit and trainers, and had a walking stick.

'Hi! Great to see you. Come on in. My parents have given me the front room.'

She hung on to the radiator in the hall as she greeted Sue, then awkwardly turning on her walking stick, she led her slowly into the front room.

It was a light and airy room with pink and cream floral wallpaper. It contained a single bed, a commode, two armchairs, and a small television on a corner table.

'Have a seat. The kids are at school. Otherwise the place would be a riot.'

'How are you getting on?' asked Sue.

'Great. I walked upstairs to the toilet today. It was a struggle, but I managed to get down again.'

'Are you still going to the hospital?' Sue asked.

'Yes, I go to rehab once a week. The physio has really helped me, and I'm having counselling there too.'

'And how are you feeling about Viktor now?' Sue tentatively asked. 'The police are still trying to find him. Jade is doing her best.'

'Well actually now I've had time to think about it all.' Liz looked down and said her words were measured and thoughtful. 'I can see a lot of it was my fault. It'll be hard, but I must forgive him when we meet again. I want to give him one more chance.'

Sue blanched.

Jenny's Story

Sue lifted the blue and white china teapot, poured herself a cup of tea, and prepared to put her feet up. She was going to watch daytime television. Something relaxing, she thought, like Famous Gardens of the World, or Scenic Swiss Railway Journeys. Anything that contrasted with the tense atmosphere in the refuge.

As she had neared the end of her shift, two residents had nearly come to blows during an argument about who could use the hairdryer first. Small matters had great significance when space and privacy were at a premium.

Sue thought how lucky she was to have her own flat. She never tired of the pleasure of being able to do everyday things without having to justify her reasons to anyone. In her past relationship with Pete, anything she did without consulting him would have been subject to criticism and the trigger for him to beat her. Her arm still twinged from time to time from where he had broken it in that final attack, before she had made her mind up to leave him for good.

Sue stretched out in her armchair.

Then the phone rang. She was tempted to ignore it but, after about a dozen rings, she gave in.

She was pleased, though, to hear Nina's voice.

'Hi Sue, are you busy?'

'No, I've just finished work, thank God. It's hell on earth here at the moment. How are you?'

'I am good, thank you, but I have a mystery here, and I wonder if you can help. Someone has got in touch with me on my website. They say a woman they know is being abused. They are worried and do not know what to do. They say they cannot mention the victim's name in case the abuser finds out.'

'I guess the person who contacted you is talking about herself.'

'Probably,' Nina agreed. 'She told me her name is Jenny, but she does not want to give any details online. It seems genuine. I do not think it will be a man pretending. Mind you, I would not put it past Viktor. He will try anything to get back at me, especially because he is still on the run. But I think it is genuine. Perhaps she will agree to meet someone in a neutral place.'

'By someone, I take it, you mean me.'

'Yes, if you can spare the time. I am worried that if we do not make personal contact with this poor woman, she will not even try asking for help again. I think she wants to meet in a quiet place. Perhaps Greenfield Park, in the rose garden by the playground. Have you ever been there? I never go out. She can make herself known to you. I think tomorrow at 4pm will suit her. Is that good for you?'

Increasingly, like Nina, Sue wanted to help women in a way that the conventional caring and legal systems would never allow. Tomorrow she would be eager to face this new challenge but, for the time being, she relaxed back into her large leather armchair. She reached for the box of chocolates and the TV remote.

The next day Sue checked the posting on Nina's website before she made her way to the park. It said, 'Can you help my friend? A man is making her do things she doesn't want to. Please private message me back.'

Outside, as she walked to the park, Sue's winter coat did little to dispel the chill she still felt after reading the posting.

Winter was giving way to spring. The sky was blue with small white clouds scudding about in the breeze. The sunlight dappled the grass that gave up the scent of its first cutting and leaves were starting to show on the trees.

In one part of the park, there was a square lawn. It was meticulously kept with a path bordered by cherry trees running all around it. A notice asked people to keep off the grass. On each side of the square was an arch that allowed entry to this formal garden. By each arch, there was a bench, and Sue sat on one of these benches.

She wondered why the suggested meeting was at this time, when children were coming out of school. Was she a school assistant, or an older student?

There was a man in his early twenties sitting on a bench across the central lawn from Sue, his face hidden by a newspaper.

On the left side of the square, a tramp was drinking from a bottle wrapped in a brown paper bag. He was unkempt with a beard, grey hair, a flat cap, dirty black trousers and heavy boots.

On the bench to the right, two young women sat together rolling pushchairs back and forth gently in front of them.

From behind Sue, groups of children were coming home from school, shouting and pulling at each other's bags. One boy grabbed a girl's bag, and then ran away across the prohibited lawn, laughing mischievously as he went, sure in the knowledge that she would not follow him.

The girls divided into two groups, one to each side of the square. They tried to catch him but he escaped through the arch opposite Sue.

Then a girl in school uniform walked slowly into the square from the same gateway as the others. She looked sullen with red eyes. Her head was down, and her rucksack was a heavy burden over her shoulder. As she came into view, the man opposite shuffled his newspaper, turned the pages, and then raised it again in front of his face.

Sue was holding a copy of 'Chat' magazine as a prearranged identifier to whoever might pass, and she saw the girl notice it.

'Are you Jenny?' Sue asked.

The girl looked about, then sat on the bench leaving a large gap between herself and Sue. Although she was blond and pretty, she had a haunted look in her eyes. She sat stiffly and looked around her. She barely glanced at the tramp and the two women. Her gaze lingered on the young man opposite who had suddenly got out his phone. He started to speak into it, whilst still concealing most of his face behind the newspaper.

'I haven't got much time,' she said with an American accent. 'My cousin might have been told to follow me.'

'Hi Jenny, I'm Sue. Tell me what seems to be the matter.'

'My step-pa is going to kill me unless I marry who he says.'

'But you're young – fifteen or so, I guess?'

'Yes. He says that if I don't agree to the marriage then he'll force me anyway.'

'What is this, an honour marriage like in Pakistan?'

'No. Brett is from the Midwest Bible belt.'

'He can't make you marry against your will.'

'He says he'll kill me if I don't. He's got my mother totally under his control since my real father died and she married him.'

'Have you lived in London for long?' Sue asked.

'My mom and I have only been here a few months. We lived in Ohio before. But as soon as my mom got married to Brett, we had to move to England. It's where The True Family is going to gather thousands more followers.'

Sue looked puzzled. 'The True Family?'

'Brett's our leader. Reverend Brett they call him. I think he's more like the Devil. He says I must marry his brother. He's about fifty. He's horrible. I'd rather die.'

'But that's illegal.'

'Those guys don't think so. All the young girls must get married about my age so they become part of The True Family. Then we never go out of the house. We are forced to have as many babies as we can. We can never have any life of our own.'

'What does your Mum think about all this?' Sue asked.

'She wants to get away too, but she's terrified. She hasn't got any money of her own. It's only men that can have money or go out. She's frightened that if I don't go ahead with the True Family marriage, something even worse will happen to me.'

'What do you mean?'

'I've heard of girls that just disappear.'

'How did it all start?'

'Brett was a new preacher that came to an old failing church in our town. He was very charismatic. He took my mom over, like he hypnotised her in some way. My brother rebelled against him. He didn't like my mother remarrying so quickly. He got work in Chicago and escaped, but I was trapped there with my mom. She was madly in love. Anyway, the church has a big infrastructure and Brett has got people he calls his brethren working for him. There are so many of these cult members that they could be anywhere.'

'How did you manage to contact us?' asked Sue.

'I used the school computer to go to Nina's website. We are not allowed to use the computer at home. Only Brett uses it and he says it is for his business only. It's all password-protected.'

Jenny was on the verge of tears. She looked away. Sue surveyed the square in silence. The two women with pushchairs were engrossed. The tramp took another swig. The face of the man across the lawn remained hidden behind the newspaper.

Sue reached out and took Jenny's hand. 'You know I run a place where women come who are scared and in trouble. You and your mum could stay for a while and we can help you sort things out. Here's my card with my mobile number. You can phone me directly any time.'

Just then, the man with the newspaper folded it and stood up.

'Oh no. It's one of the brethren,' whispered Jenny.

He glanced at them, then turned to look behind him.

The next second, a middle-aged man joined him in the garden. Ignoring the 'Keep off the Grass' sign, the two men swaggered together over the lawn towards them.

'Hi, Jenny! How goes it?' the second man called.

'It's him,' Jenny muttered to Sue.

'Howdy! I'm Brett Chandler! Glad to meet you!'

Sue took his hand out of politeness. It was a firm handshake. Too firm, almost aggressive.

'Aren't you going to introduce me to your friend, Jenny?' he asked, still holding Sue's hand.

Jenny kept silent, so Sue said, 'Hello, I'm Sue Barlow from Social Services,' and finally extricated her hand.

'Oh, Social Services. Very good. There's nothing wrong, I hope?'

The man who had been reading the newspaper cocked an eyebrow and echoed, 'Nothing wrong, we hope?'

'Oh no, Mr Chandler. Jenny was just telling me about her life at home and your church.'

His eyes lit up. 'Call me Brett, please. A wonderful Christian movement it is too, The True Family. Tell me, Sue, are you a religious person?'

'Well, not exactly, I suppose you'd say I was an open believer – I believe in them all.'

'Oh well. That's a mighty fine statement you've made there, I do declare. Yes, mighty fine.'

Brett searched Sue's eyes and then narrowed his focus on Sue's left cheek as though he'd found something. He concentrated on that spot as he said 'Well, perhaps you'd like to come to our church on Sunday, since you're so interested in my daughter. I'd be pleased to introduce you to the rest of The True Family.'

Sue turned to Jenny, who was looking downcast, her hands clasped in her lap.

'Thank you, Brett, But I can't make it this Sunday. Perhaps in the future?'

'Right you are there, lady. As regards Jenny, I think that we can take care of our own issues. We don't need Social Services, but you'd be welcome to come and worship with us. By the way, how is it that you came upon us?'

'I was asked by the school to talk to Jenny,' Sue waffled.

'Oh, were you? Well let me assure you that the schoolteacher, or whoever it was, has the wrong idea about our Jenny here. She's no problems at school. Have you, Jenny, heh? Just got a vivid imagination, that's all.' He prodded her for a response. 'No problems.'

Still with her eyes down, Jenny muttered something inaudible.

'Come on, Jenny,' said Brett. 'Let's see what Eileen's cooking at home. Growing girl like you has to eat as much as she can.'

He put an arm around Jenny and hauled her away.

After they had gone a few yards, he called back to Sue, 'Bye now. You take care.'

He mimed the action of shooting a gun playfully at her.

They left by one of the arches at the side. The man with the newspaper followed.

As Sue watched them go, Jenny turned back and mouthed something like 'Help me', but her stepfather tugged her away, through the archway, and then they were gone.

Sue sat alone on the bench for some time, thinking about her encounter with Jenny. Her claims were extreme. Surely, something like this would have been picked up at school. Weren't teachers vigilant for any signs of child abuse these days? She wondered if professionals might be reluctant to ask too many searching questions because Jenny came from a different cultural background.

On the other hand, perhaps Brett really was telling the truth about Jenny's vivid imagination and he had already arranged some psychological help.

That evening Sue phoned Nina from the refuge and told her she had met up with Jenny.

Nina said, 'Brett Chandler? I am looking now... Ah yes, it is coming up.... Uh oh. He is trouble. He has abused many people in his church in America. He believes God has sent him here to convert people. He has been here too long for his visa. If caught, he will be deported. He has child abuse allegations to face in America.'

'Huh,' said Sue. 'Sounds like a nasty piece of work.'

'Also, the cult specialises in arranging false marriages. I bet that his marriage to Eileen, Jenny's mother, is probably one. Null and void, so he will have no grounds of appeal.'

'I'm not surprised. I'll give the school a ring tomorrow and fix up a meeting. The allegations are so serious I need to check out what they know.'

The secondary school was an anonymous grey flat-roofed building from the 1960's. Sue opened the swing doors and walked down the long corridor to the Head Teacher's office. Why, she thought, do all schools have that same smell, the one she remembered from her childhood? And being sent to the Head Teacher's office – that was very familiar too. Sue had been a bit of a rebel when she was in her teens. She smiled, as she looked down at the length of her skirt now – these days a respectable 'just below the knee.'

Miss Prentice, the head teacher, gave Sue a faint frosty smile.

'I understand you have some concerns about Jenny Chandler?'

Sue outlined her conversation with Jenny the previous day.

'Yes, we are fully aware of Jenny's strange ideas about her family,' said Miss Prentice. 'Her stepfather let us know as soon as she started here a few months ago. He is a wonderful man...a deeply committed Christian... and it must be terrible for him to be the target of Jenny's paranoid thinking. She doesn't say much here but Brett told me that she thinks he is a cult leader who wants her to marry his brother. He is prepared to pay for her to have the very best private psychiatric treatment.'

'Have you met Jenny's mother?' Sue asked.

'No, she is not at all well. Brett says she has motor neurone disease, and he has to do practically everything for her. He comes to the school to meet with me every week to check on Jenny's progress. He has even volunteered to run a religious knowledge discussion group for our year 11 students. If only more parents were so caring.'

'Thank you, Miss Prentice. That's very reassuring news.' Sue stood up and shook hands with her, but Sue knew that the true story was very different.

As she left the school, children were starting to stream out of their classrooms and down the corridor for the break. Sue was swept up in their energy. Surrounded by students she burst out the swing doors, free, into the fresh spring morning.

After lunch at the refuge, Sue got the box of toys off the shelf to amuse two toddlers that she was babysitting while their mother kept an appointment at the job centre. They were drawing matchstick people and houses, when Sue's mobile rang.

Sue could just hear the quiet voice of a young girl on the other end.

'Hello, Jenny? Is that you? Speak up. I can't hear you. What's the matter?'

'I can't speak any louder. Brett won't let me use the phone. I borrowed this from a girl at school. I…What?'

There was a noise of a scuffle, then shouting. Sue recognised Brett Chandler's voice and then the phone went dead.

In a state of panic, Sue phoned Jade.

Jade asked, 'Do you really think there's been some violence?'

'Yes, and she says that she must marry this man who they've got lined up for her, and if she doesn't then they'll kill her.'

'Then the police should be involved. I'll meet you at the house.'

When Sue arrived, Jade was already inside with her police team. There were broken vases and an upturned table. Jenny was sitting in an armchair crying and bleeding from the nose. Jenny's mother was picking up pieces of the broken vases from the floor. It was evident that she was not the invalid that Brett Chandler had described.

Chandler was in handcuffs and sitting on the sofa in the lounge. He spluttered, 'You'll never get away with this, I'm warning you. I'll get my lawyer on the job. This is police harassment. Just because we have different religious beliefs.'

'My sources tell me,' began Sue, careful not to reveal whom she was talking about, 'that there has been child abuse and a lack of care for others here. Some religion, this is!'

'Come on, let's go, Chandler.' Jade ordered. She and the other officers led him away.

'The rest of Brett's True Family will be angry about this and might take it out on us,' Jenny's mother, Eileen, confided to Sue after the police had left. Putting an arm around Jenny, she added, 'I don't know where we can go to be safe.'

'Look,' said Sue to Jenny and her mother, 'I think it's best if you come to stay at the refuge for a few days.'

Some weeks later, Eileen's marriage certificate was found to be a forgery. She had been tricked and the document had no validity in law.

Brett Chandler was deported to face serious charges of exploitation and child abuse back in Ohio.

When she heard this news, Eileen cried with joy. 'I've been thinking about how bad he is – he's really shown another side I didn't know about. Evil. This latest thing with Jenny has brought it all home to me. I'm so glad that the marriage licence is a sham. He had me really believing in him. However, I suppose that's Brett Chandler. I'm glad I've got no ties to him now. I've decided that Jenny and I will go back to America to my parents' home on the West Coast. The cult can't reach us there. Thanks a million for helping us escape. I'll never forget what you have done for Jenny and me.'

Sue kissed them goodbye on the last day of their stay in the refuge and watched them get in a taxi to the airport. She promised to keep in touch, certain that they would be going to a better life back home in America. Free, and with the real family who loved them.

Later, Sue called to see Liz at her parent's house. She had made tremendous progress over the past few weeks. She still used a stick, but could now manage stairs quite well, and had even ventured outside for a short stroll down the street.

'Well, you are having some real success stories at work,' Liz congratulated Sue. 'Mother and daughter reunited. That's wonderful. I wish I could help people like you do.'

'Why not? If you like, you could volunteer and help us out with some filing at the refuge. It would be much appreciated. Me and Cath, my deputy, are up to our eyes in paperwork with all the new rules and regulations they keep bringing in.'

'Yes. I'd like that. In fact, I can come next Monday.'

'That would be great,' said Sue.

Sue still felt guilty about not having done more to dissuade Liz from going back to Viktor last year. Lately, she had become worried that Liz was developing a positive attitude towards him again. She was pleased that she would have this extra contact with Liz. Perhaps it would give her the opportunity to talk to her more about a future without Viktor.

Wanda's Story

Sue had just finished her weekly shop in the supermarket. Although she usually enjoyed shopping, today was much more of a toil than a pleasure. Her trolley was piled high with value brand cereals, pasta, and bread, all of which she bought in bulk for the refuge. She was exhausted. The final straw was having to rummage through her handbag for the money-off vouchers. She felt the eyes of impatient people behind her in the queue. She muttered to herself when she realised that once again she had left the vouchers piled up on the window ledge at home. Sue was pretty sure they would be out of date by her next visit.

The supermarket café was packed, but Sue thought she must have a break before driving back to the refuge. She parked her trolley where she could easily see it and joined the queue for hot drinks.

Some of the customers at the tables were familiar types. Two women with shopping bags and pushchairs. A bloke with a notebook and pen studying a racing paper. A young man in a suit gulping a sandwich.

Sue carried her coffee around the crowded café hoping to find a table to herself but each one was taken. Eventually she found one with just a single occupant, a young woman in her late twenties, staring into her coffee. Sue could just relax and read her newspaper without any need to make polite conversation. As she turned the pages, she glanced briefly at the woman seated across from her.

She had long dark hair tied tightly back in a ponytail and was wearing large gold hoop earrings. Her face was covered in heavy tan makeup.

Sue sipped her coffee and, out of the corner of her eye, took a more searching look. Even the woman's amount of makeup could not hide the telltale signs of old bruising on her cheeks and what seemed to be a recent scar above her left eye. Her hunched appearance suggested she was in pain.

Sue finished her coffee and smiled as she left the table.

There was no response.

As Sue drove away from the supermarket, she thought about what might have caused those injuries.

The next Sunday, Sue was in the supermarket café again. It was less crowded than her last visit, and she managed to get a table to herself. She put her carrier bag on the seat opposite and looked back to the queue at the serving area. She saw the woman who had been sitting with her last week. This time she looked more relaxed, and she was walking and moving easily. She noticed Sue, smiled in recognition, and came over to her table.

Sue moved her bag, so the woman could sit down.

'Hello,' said Sue. 'I saw you here last week. How are you?'

'Much better than I was, thanks. I was in a lot of pain last week, but most of it has worn off and I can get out and about now. Not that I get to go out much.'

'Oh, why's that?'

'Well it's a long story, but I'm having to live in a women's refuge.'

Sue sensed that the woman wanted to talk, as many do who have kept so much to themselves in their troubled relationships.

'Has it helped being there?'

'A bit. At least there has been no news or any sign of Rob, my ex, so that's a real blessing.'

'Do you think he'll try to find you?' Sue asked.

'He'll try alright. But I've made my mind up this time. I'll never ever go back to him.'

Sue leaned forward and quietly asked, 'Were you with Rob for long?'

'Nearly six years. I met him when I had just turned twenty-one. He swept me off my feet. I mean I had been out with other lads, but he was different. He was older, in his thirties, and so good-looking. He dressed well too. I couldn't believe my luck. Then the romance. Each day he would send me flowers or a poem. When we first moved in together it was wonderful. He said I was his perfect woman. We didn't need anybody else in the world.'

'I understand what you've been through. I work in a refuge. My name's Sue.'

'Hi, I'm Wanda.'

Wanda was clearly interested as Sue continued. 'The women in our refuge have similar stories. They are all recovering from damaging relationships.'

'Damaging? Huh!' Wanda's voice was louder. 'I'd damage him if I could, but I know that he'd get back at me.'

Sue nodded, and took a sip of coffee.

'After all he did to me,' said Wanda. 'First, he said that I was the only person he ever loved and that he would stay with me forever. Then one night he lost his temper and called me horrible names. In the morning, he said he was sorry and it would never happen again. Like a fool, I believed him. He bought me flowers to make up for it. But then little things started to build into a pattern. Whenever I did anything good, like painting the house, he criticised me even though I did it well. When I tried to explain to him how I felt, he just couldn't see it. He said I was crazy, and that he was easy-going and tolerant of me. Tolerant of <u>me</u>!'

Wanda put her head in her hands and looked at her coffee cup. Once she had collected herself, she continued, 'In the end I began to feel that I was responsible for everything that went wrong. But I stayed with him because I thought that it might work out OK in the end.'

She shrugged.

'Then it got really bad. Each time we quarrelled, he hit me. Each time I thought it was about something different, and it seemed justified – yes, that's it – justified. I began to agree with him that he was in the right. Still, he never did it in public – he was calm and polite, and our friends liked him. They never knew the truth. I was good at covering up my bruises, and he was good at not being a bully in company.'

Her tears welled up, and Wanda rummaged amongst the makeup in her handbag to find a tissue.

'In the end, I was always on edge, always in the wrong. Whenever I tried to do anything to put it right, I was beaten up. I felt I deserved it. I felt it was all my own fault. My life changed. Bit by bit I stopped going out with friends. In the end, I even stopped visiting my family. Rob liked the house to be clean and tidy and he wanted me to be there for him when he came home from work. I was always busy, but I did think I could do something more. So, I enrolled on a care course at college. He went mad when I told him. I had never seen anyone in a rage like that. It terrified me. As usual he said he was sorry afterwards.'

Wanda dabbed her eyes with the tissue again.

'But he carried on finding fault. Saucepans were in the wrong place, the towels in the bathroom weren't folded neatly. He started to criticise my appearance. I couldn't do right. If I was tired and hadn't put makeup on, then he said I was lazy and couldn't be bothered to look nice for him. If I dressed up, he said I looked like a tart. I said if he felt like that, then he would be better off if I left. However, he told me I couldn't manage on my own. I was useless. Do you know, after a while I started to believe that too. I lost everything that was ever me.'

Sue leaned across the table and gently touched Wanda's hand.

Wanda drew a deep breath and continued. 'For the last two years I felt I was living with a monster. I could never relax... even in bed. I was walking on eggshells every minute Rob was with me. The slightest thing sent him into a fury. He would hit or kick me continually. If we were out he could keep his anger in for a while, but I knew he would start on me as soon as we got home. In the past, he apologised but then he just seemed to carry on as if nothing had happened. This last time I had to go to hospital because the injuries were so bad. I saw a social worker there and she gave me the address of the refuge I'm at now. She said it had not been open long. So, one day I just packed my bags and left. I literally ran away from my own life.'

Wanda took a sip of her coffee.

'At first, it was great in the hostel. The other women were supportive. They had all been through similar things to me. It seemed much better than where I had come from. It just seemed strange that a man ran it. There was a woman there as well. She was his deputy. I don't know what happened to her. She left after a couple of weeks. Then there was a succession of deputies. Bill, the manager, found fault with each of them. I heard him shouting. I thought it was something to do with me. It reminded me of when I was back with Rob. I thought it must be me! It must be me!'

At this, Wanda broke down in tears. Sue reached across the table and held her hand again as she continued.

'And there's another thing. I'm getting worried about the place in general. The other girls have told me that quite a few women seem to have gone missing in the last few weeks. There seems to be a pattern to it. Bill is generally pretty horrible to everybody, but sometimes he starts to be nice to one of the women, then he invites a couple of them to his flat for meals. After that, they get moved to a better room at the top of the building. Then we don't see them again. Most of the girls are originally from Eastern Europe. Bill says he has arranged accommodation and better work for them in their own country and they have gone back home. But there is something funny about it. I just can't believe it.'

'I know how you feel,' said Sue. 'I've been in a bad relationship too. In my refuge there are no men. If you like, you can think about coming to mine if your place doesn't work out. You would be more than welcome. We are fairly quiet at the moment, so you could have plenty of space for yourself.'

She gave Wanda her phone number, and told her the general area where the refuge was. As they drank their coffee Sue told Wanda more about the refuge and the things they could do to support her if she wanted.

'You are so kind,' Wanda said. 'Thank you so much. I

would be really grateful if I could move to your refuge. I would have to let Bill know that I'm going, though. He says that we must give him a few days' notice if we are leaving so that he can do all the paperwork to get our benefits changed.' Wanda looked at the phone number Sue had given her. 'I'll ring you in a few days to let you know when I'm moving.'

Sue gave Wanda a lift back to the area where she was staying. It was not far from the supermarket. Huge tower blocks were being built in what was previously a run-down area. It would soon provide flats and offices for well-off London business people. There was a price to pay though, Sue thought, in the loss of community and care for neighbours.

A few of the old buildings were still standing. Some of the windows of the flats that made up a three-storey building were boarded up, and it was hard to imagine that anyone was living there. Sue pulled up at the end of the street.

'This is fine here,' Wanda said. 'I'm told I mustn't let people drop me outside because we have to keep the exact location secret. I can walk from here. It's a pretty grim area, isn't it? I'm staying in one of the basement preparation rooms in an old butcher's shop. It's a bit like something out of a horror film. Still, it's better than where I was before.'

The two women said their goodbyes and agreed to meet in the cafe the next week.

Sue watched Wanda walk down to what once had been a thriving butcher's shop. Now the shop front glass was dusty, and the paintwork was peeling. The display slabs for meat were still there, cracked and dirty.

Wanda rang a bell. The door was held open by a stocky man in his forties. He smiled at Wanda, and looked up the street towards Sue in her car. Sue noted that smile. He showed both upper and lower teeth, but his eyes were cold. It was a parody of a smile. Sue shuddered.

As she drove off, Sue said to herself, 'This is either my vivid imagination, or there is something very wrong going on here.'

Sue tried to make enquiries about the background of this new refuge. She asked her boss in the Social Services office who said that there was an application for one but it had not yet been formally approved.

Mystified, Sue rang Jade. 'Do you know anything about a new refuge that has been set up? Or do the police have a number or an address for it?'

Jade phoned her back later that day. 'No, I can't find anything about it. Nobody's mentioned it. It must be very new. Strange that Social Services don't know much about it, or they won't tell you.'

'Yes, very strange. Anyway, thanks for looking, Jade.'

The next week Sue waited at the café as usual, but Wanda didn't show.

Sue decided to drive over to have a closer look at the refuge from the outside. She parked and casually walked down the street. On the doorstep of the old butcher's shop, something caught her eye. She bent down to examine it more closely. It was a gold hoop earring like Wanda's.

There was no sign of life in the house, but she rang the bell.

No answer.

She was about to give up, but as she turned to go she heard a tapping coming from above. She looked up and saw Wanda's frightened face pressed against an upper window. Suddenly a man's hand clutched Wanda from behind and pulled her away.

Sue hammered on the door.

'Wanda!' she shouted.

There was no reply.

She pulled out her phone and dialled Jade.

'Look, that refuge we were talking about, I'm outside it. I'm sure there's a man holding a woman prisoner in there.'

'Are you sure?'

'Yes. I've seen it with my own eyes.'

'OK, Sue, we're on our way,' said Jade, 'We'll be with you in a few minutes. Just stay where you are. Don't go in.'

But as soon as she had rung off Sue heard a scream from the upper room.

'Wanda!' shouted Sue.

She looked up and then heard Wanda scream again and a man shout, 'You bitch, I'll kill you.'

Sue didn't hesitate. She saw a half-brick by next door's dustbin.

She smashed it against the door lock. The door gave way easily.

Still holding the half-brick, she ran inside.

The place was half-derelict, fusty, with wallpaper peeling off the walls.

She ran along dirty bare floorboards, shouting 'Wanda!'

A scuffling noise came from an upper room.

She raced up the stairs, with the brick still in her hand.

'Get out or I'll kill her!' a man's voice shouted from behind a first-floor door.

Enraged, Sue found strength to kick the door open. In the middle of the room were a table and two metal chairs arranged as if for an interview. Behind these by the window across the other side of the room, a man was holding Wanda in front of him with a knife to her throat.

'Get back, bitch, or I'll kill her!'

Sue threw the brick at the window behind him. It was a good shot. As the glass shattered he staggered forwards in shock. Wanda wrenched herself free.

Sue picked up one of the metal chairs and hit him across the head.

He collapsed, dropping the knife.

Wanda picked up the other chair and thrust it at him as he clutched the table and tried to get up.

He rolled onto his back.

Wanda hit him again across the face.

He made a gurgling sound and lost consciousness.

Wanda fell into Sue's arms, and shook in a fit of tears.

As Sue held Wanda, she became aware of muffled banging and shouting coming from below.

'He's locked them all in the cellar,' Wanda said.

They ran downstairs and slid back the bolt on the cellar head door. Four frightened women came cautiously out.

'Don't worry – you're safe now,' Sue reassured them.

'We've dealt with him.'

Police sirens heralded Jade's appearance with other officers through the front door.

The police searched the unconscious man. He was Russian. His real name was Boris Dubrovsky. They found a pocket notebook on him containing details of women he had sold for prostitution.

Wanda said that she would have been next. Women who didn't co-operate with him were never seen again.

'You'd better come to stay in my refuge today after we've given a statement to the police,' Sue told Wanda.

Wanda hugged Sue as tears of relief and gratitude came to her eyes.

The other women who had been held captive were offered places in refuges across town by Social Services.

Wanda settled into Sue's refuge knowing she could make positive plans for her future. Finally, she was in a safe place where she could recover from years of being stripped of her identity and go forward to being her own person again.

Sue was working on management records on her laptop when the door opened, and Liz came in carrying a tray of iced fairy cakes.

'Would you like one, Sue?'

Liz put the tray down slowly and carefully. She was still having some problems coordinating movements and Sue noticed that some of the white icing on the cakes had run onto the paper cases.

Sue took one. 'They're lovely,' she said between mouthfuls.

'Just like I used to make when my husband Frank was alive,' said Liz. 'I think about him a lot now. He was wonderful with the kids.'

'They were his children of course. Do they remember him?'

'Yes, but I'm not sure how much. Viktor never wanted me to even mention Frank. He just said, "He's dead – forget him. The kids are mine now." I will be able to talk to Heather and

Toby about their real Dad from now on.'

'That's good.'

'I was thinking of taking them to see his grave, but I haven't got the car of course since Viktor took ours. I'm looking forward to getting my licence back. I've tried my Dad's car.'

'How did that go?'

'I can't control the pedals properly yet. I haven't got the strength in my legs. I hope I'll be able to do it soon.'

'I'm sure you will.'

'Yes, then when I get more active I'll be able to really do more around here. I could even help you set up another branch of the refuge. That would be great, wouldn't it?'

Sue did not reply. She just stared back in disbelief.

Sue's Story

S ue had just returned home after visiting Wanda, a former
resident who was now settled in her nice little flat on the
high street. Wanda had already made friends with her new
neighbours. Sue was impressed by how well she had recovered
from her ordeal at the bogus refuge. She had enrolled on a
college course and it looked as if she was going to pass with
flying colours.

Sue liked to follow up former residents to make sure
things were going well for them. Some other refuges never
bothered, just dumping ex-residents in a distant area with only a
quick phone call after a few weeks. But Sue had a different
approach. She liked visiting these women and it gave her a warm
feeling of satisfaction. Today, after seeing how Wanda was
rebuilding her life, she was in a good mood as she returned to her
flat on the top floor of the refuge.

Once inside the hall she closed the door behind her and
leaned against it, reflecting on another job well done. Now she
could relax in the comfort of her own little flat where everything
was in its place.

However, today there was a slight chill in the living
room that she could not explain. The window was closed. So, the
cold air must be coming from somewhere else.

She put her hand on the bedroom doorknob and turned it to open the door. A gust of cold air stung her face from the open French window.

Instantly she sprang back into the hall and opened the kitchen door. That room was warm, exactly as she had left it.

Sue looked around the flat. In the kitchen drawer her bankcard and bank statement were still there.

On the table in the lounge, the magazine pile was as untidy as she had left it. The top one scruffily folded, and still open on the page she had been reading. The dregs in the coffee cup were undisturbed.

Everything seemed as normal, just as she usually expected to find on returning from one of her outings. Except the unexplained open French window.

Cautiously she went back into the bedroom. The French window opened onto a small balcony and a fire escape. Sue seldom used the balcony as it overlooked a busy road full of traffic fumes.

She looked out. The street was empty with no sign of anything unusual.

She worked the handle to check the locking mechanism. Then, as a trial, she left it closed as she had done when she went out. She tapped it with her hand experimentally to see if the wind might have dislodged it. It was secure.

She looked around and then saw something she could not explain. There was a small bump under the sheet that covered her pillow. She drew back the cover to reveal an object that she thought at first was a small dead bird. When she looked at it more closely, she saw it was a bundle of black feathers tied together with string.

Someone had been inside her flat and put that thing in her bed.

Sue felt a wave of panic. Was it her ex-partner, Pete? He could be capable of anything. The last she had heard he had gone to live with relatives in Northern Ireland. That was five years ago, but she had always feared that one day he would find her. He had told her, when they were together, that she belonged to him and that he would never let her go.

Feeling physically sick, she ran down the stairs to her

office in the basement. She dialled the local police station and asked for Jade.

'Jade, I'm sorry to bother you at work, but I think Pete's found me. He's actually been inside my place. I'm so frightened. I don't know what to do.'

'Don't worry. Sit tight. It's a police matter now. I'll be with you soon.'

By the time Jade arrived at the refuge, Sue had calmed down a little. She took Jade up to her flat and showed her the open French window leading to the balcony.

Jade picked up the bunch of feathers and studied it. 'God knows what this is. They usually break in and take stuff. Not leave it behind.'

She looked all around the flat with Sue. Nothing had been taken.

'I think it's just someone off the street who saw the door open up here,' said Jade. 'Are you absolutely sure you locked it? If not then they've taken the opportunity to get in and have a look round to see if there is anything valuable to nick.'

Sue, who had recovered from her initial shock, joked. 'Well I haven't got anything like that. I'm still waiting for someone to give me diamonds.'

'I really don't think it was Pete,' Jade reassured Sue. 'I think he would be a lot more direct in his approach. From what I've seen here, and this thing....' She picked up the feathered object. 'I reckon it's an old-style vagrant, maybe a mental health case. They keep lots of crazy stuff like this and God knows why they put them where they do. Maybe you disturbed him when you came back home this evening.'

Jade's calm and logical explanation of what might have happened made total sense to Sue. There was no way Pete would have been that subtle. He would have just waited for her to come into the flat, and then used his fists the minute he set eyes on her. She had a quick coffee with Jade, changed the bed linen then settled down in bed for an early night.

In the middle of the night, Sue awoke and turned over in bed to peer at the illuminated alarm clock. It was 4.30am. She shut her eyes and tried to make her mind a blank. But thoughts and images crowded into her head.

She saw herself ten years ago, frightened and weeping as she sat in the accident and emergency department trying to find words to tell the social worker how she came to have a broken arm. In the past, she had explained her frequent injuries as being down to her own clumsiness when she had fallen or bumped into things. The truth was she had been married to a vicious monster and she had been too frightened to break free.

She remembered holding her hands up to protect her face from Pete's fists, and collapsing on the floor as kicks rained on her stomach. At that time, she thought she would die from the attacks.

But Sue drew comfort from the fact that these terrible memories were fading over time. Once she had found courage to ask for help she had received wonderful support from refuge staff and a counsellor. She left her old life behind, moving far from her home in Scotland to London, and for the past eight years she had managed this refuge herself. She loved her job and wanted to give something back for all the help that others had given her.

Eventually Sue fell asleep.

The next day the break-in was still on her mind. Even though Jade had reassured her, Sue could not stop racking her brain for an explanation. She could not believe that she had left her French windows unlocked for so many days. And what type of vagrant would climb up the fire escape to leave something on her pillow? She wondered if they had somehow managed to get a key.

She attempted to catch up with the paperwork for a forthcoming inspection of the refuge. It seemed that paperwork was all the inspectors were interested in. Something they could check and criticise. They did not care that she was so short-staffed there was no one free to sit down to talk with the victims of abuse. The inspectors were not worried that funding was so reduced that even toilet paper had to be rationed and all food had to be bought from the supermarket's 'value' range.

Finally, at eight o'clock that evening, she thankfully climbed the stairs to her flat.

She slept well and awoke refreshed the next morning, but over the next days and weeks, doubts kept surfacing in her mind. She even started to have a vague feeling that she was being followed in the street. Worst of all, she was no longer totally at ease in her flat. Her precious sense of safety in her new life away from Pete had been destroyed.

She shared these feelings with her friends Jade and Nina who were always there for her, and willing to listen. They tried their best to reassure her.

However, Sue became more fearful as time went on. She wondered if this was what it was like to lose your mind, because increasingly the paranoid thoughts were taking over her life. She avoided going out and tried to spend as much time as she could in the refuge office, rather than going up to her flat.

The stress was apparent in her physical appearance. She lost weight and her face became pale and drawn, so that the other staff and women at the refuge worried about her health, and were building up to asking her what was wrong.

One afternoon, some weeks after the break-in, Sue was so exhausted that she fell asleep at her desk. When she woke up she said to herself, 'Enough is enough. I've got to pull myself together.'

With this thought in mind, she purposefully climbed the stairs to her flat and went straight to the bathroom.

Sue decided she would have a shower and then change and go out to visit Nina. She must reclaim her life. Surely, her unreal fears were connected to things that had happened in the past. She was determined to put all that behind her.

The shower was warm and relaxing and, as Sue let the water flow over her, it seemed to wash away all her anxieties.

She wrapped herself in a large soft white towel and made her way into her bedroom to get her fresh clothes.

But, as soon as she entered the room, she froze in horror. Lying on the pillow was a chicken's foot, recently severed. There was a clear bloodstain on the white pillowcase.

Sue ran back into the bathroom and locked the door. She

struggled to put her old clothes back on as she was shaking so much. When she had managed to get dressed she opened the door a crack and listened intently in case the intruder was still somewhere in the flat.

As she heard nothing, she raced the short distance through the hall and slammed her door behind her. She ran down the refuge stairs and out into the street.

She just ran and ran.

Nina's flat was about a mile away, but Sue didn't stop for a moment as she raced towards it.

She hammered on the door and rang the bell at the same time.

Sue was relieved beyond belief to hear Nina's familiar Russian accent through the intercom.

The front door clicked open and she hurried up the stairs to Nina's flat.

The flat door was open and Nina was in her usual place in front of her array of computer monitors. She turned and immediately saw that Sue was in a terrible state.

'Sit down. What has happened?'

Sue slumped into the chair next to Nina. Now she was in a safe place she felt the full impact of what she had seen. She sobbed uncontrollably.

Nina put her arm around her. 'Hey, you are safe now. Tell me about it.'

Sue managed to describe the thing on her pillow. Although it was only a chicken's foot, it held a nightmare sense of horror and menace that Sue had never felt before.

Nina responded, 'This is not your mind playing tricks Sue. It is nothing to do with your past. Someone has managed to get into your flat and has deliberately left a Voodoo charm that they think will harm you.'

'That sounds like something from a horror film. It's terrible.' Sue started to cry again.

'No!' Nina replied confidently. 'This is good. Now we know a real person is doing this bad thing. It is not just your imagination. Can you think of anyone who would want to scare you or would even think of using Voodoo? If you are sure you have locked it, then they must have a key to come up the fire escape and open the balcony door. Maybe someone in the refuge from years ago.'

Sue racked her brains. So many women had passed through the refuge in the eight years she had been there, but she couldn't think of a likely suspect.

'Well then. Let us look at the dates. Perhaps it is an anniversary of something in the past. The first date was when...?'

'August twenty-first. A few weeks ago.'

'And the second date?'

'Today. September twenty-third.'

'OK. Can you send me admission and leaving dates for your residents since the refuge opened, including those before you came?'

'Yes. I can easily look those up.'

Sue went back to the office and emailed the details to Nina.

Within an hour, Nina had analysed the figures, and phoned Sue.

'There is one person with a Caribbean-sounding name whose admission and discharge dates match up exactly with your break-ins, but it is from years ago. So, it could be an anniversary. She is called Olivia Williams.'

'Oh yes, I remember now. My old manager from where I used to work in Social Services told me about the case of a woman who came from New Orleans. She'd lost everything after Hurricane Katrina and came to live with her sister over here. But her brother-in-law started to make advances towards her. He even made love charms and spells to control her. One night he came into her room and tried to rape her. She managed to get free and came to stay at the refuge. But that was before my time. My flat was used by residents then.'

'Where is this woman now?'

'God knows. I don't think we'll find her. Last I heard she was going to America, but she might have come back to this area.'

'If she is back then she could be in danger. She could be the target, not you. A man who would hold a grudge for so long could be very dangerous. We need to find him. If we knew the general area I could do a street cam search, but it would take weeks.'

'Yes,' Sue agreed. 'But the police aren't interested. They think it's just a minor break-in.'

'Well, perhaps it is not. What about the man, do you have a record of his name?'

'No. We didn't really keep detailed records then, but you might be able to get his name from court cases around that time.'

'OK. I will search court cases with Caribbean names – maybe for violence or GBH for those dates. It is a long shot, but it could be that there is a record of violence on the very night Olivia came to the refuge.'

'It's worth a try.'

'Perhaps after all these years he has been able to track down the refuge. Have you been out in public, giving more talks, for instance? People with grudges might have been in the audience. Think hard. Do you remember any strange characters?'

'Do you mean that he might come after me?'

'I think he would plant a charm, not to get at you, but to put some voodoo on the woman you helped even though she left the refuge long ago.'

'Ugh!'

'He might try to put the charm in the place where she stayed.'

'And my flat was a part of the refuge he could get in unnoticed?'

'Yes. If he was skilful, as we think he might be. He might even hope that you will send her the charm. Some hope! But if you did pass it on, and she is a believer, then she would freak out.'

Nina hung up, keen to get back to her data search.

Sue shuddered. Even though the refuge had helped many women in the past, some had problems that continued to haunt them for years afterwards.

Nina rang back a couple of hours later.

'Bingo,' Nina said. 'There is a Churchill Winston Abellard living not far from you. He was done for GBH seven years ago for assaults on the same dates as your break-ins. I bet it is him. If it is, then he needs to be warned off.'

'Well, maybe we can't prove it, but I feel so angry about this. I feel like breaking into his place and leaving something for him to find. Something to freak him out. Let's see how he likes that.'

'That is an idea. As we say in Russia, the prey can become the trapper. But you must be careful. I know the police's hands are tied. They will treat what you are going to do as a crime if they find out. They might even prosecute you. Do not get caught. Even our very own friend Sergeant Jade might have to run you in.'

'She is a friend, but there are lines she can't cross, I suppose.'

'Here is the address. Acacia Street.'

Next day Sue drove around to Acacia Street. She walked up the alley behind the terraced houses to the address Nina had given her. The back gate was rickety. She looked over and saw the back window. Its curtains were drawn, but there was a catch on the sash window which could easily be forced with a knife.

Sue drove back to the refuge and worked out a plan.

Weeks passed.

Sue rang Nina who said that she would watch the front of the house on the street webcam, and could also cover the derelict alleyway if Sue temporarily propped up an old camera phone on the back gate.

Sue googled images and constructed a small grotesque doll using cloth and wire into the shape of a man. She could hardly believe that she was doing this. It was almost as if she was in a dream, especially when she inserted a needle through its heart.

On her return to Acacia Street, she crept into the back yard of the terraced house, flicked the latch to the window and opened it. She tossed the doll into the room. In that instant, she smelt an appalling stench that came from it. She was almost sick as she rushed out of the backyard, leaving the window open.

Over the next few days, Sue relaxed. There were no more incidents of break-ins at the refuge. Sue was pleased in the knowledge that she had presumably scared the intruder off.

Then she had a phone call from Jade.

'I don't want to alarm you but there still seems to be someone going about the neighbourhood breaking in and leaving voodoo dolls. A local man with GBH form has been the latest victim. In Acacia Street. I don't suppose any of your residents had any contact with him at all. Or if you know anything?'

'No. We've not had any contact with that part of town.'

'I thought so. Anyway, it's a strange case. The bloke hadn't been seen for some time. He was found dead by a local community police officer after reports of a strange smell coming from his flat. Turned out to be his body. Been dead for weeks! Natural causes, apparently, a heart attack. Next to the body was a voodoo doll with a pin through its heart. He could have been the man who was making these things, or a believer frightened to death by one. Perhaps, it was nothing to do with that at all, and he just died naturally. So watch out, there might still be a voodoo stalker about.'

'Oh, thanks, Jade. Still, I haven't had anything happen for weeks. I think whoever it was must have moved on.'

Sue recounted the tale of Churchill Winston Abellard to Liz, as they sorted through paperwork in the refuge office.

'Abellard harboured a grudge for years and would go to any lengths to get revenge,' Sue explained. 'I didn't feel safe even in my own flat.'

'It must have been terrible for you. He deserved to die. Somebody like that. Totally evil.'

Sue saw Liz's eyes flash with anger at the thought of Abellard, and she wondered what Liz felt about Viktor now.

Some weeks ago, she had spoken about forgiving him.

'So what do you think about Viktor now? Do you still believe that you were in any way to blame for what he did to you?'

'No. I don't. I'm having counselling. I realise that he did terrible things to me and that was his fault completely. I was the victim then. But not any longer, believe me.'

Viktor's Story

The police had given up their intensive hunt for Viktor, but Jade was always on the alert for any information about him. Nina also kept in touch with her contacts in Europe to try to locate this evil man. Liz's ordeal was not going to be forgotten so easily, and she would get justice.

Eventually the women's persistence paid off. Before fleeing the scene of the attack, Viktor had callously searched through Liz's bag as she lay on the floor and had stolen all her bankcards. Credit card theft was not a top priority at the busy inner-city police station where Jade worked, but she had taken the trouble to keep checking regularly to see if any of the cards had been traced. Rather than stopping them, the bank had agreed to put a low withdrawal limit on the cards to keep them active, as a bait to catch Viktor.

Sure enough, after almost a year, a card was reported as having been used in a cash machine a short distance from Newcastle.

Jade got hold of the CCTV footage of the street at the time of the cash withdrawal. She copied the footage onto a DVD and took it around to Nina's flat to play to her and Sue.

Nina had been uncertain about letting someone into her home that she did not know in person. However, Sue had managed to persuade her to let Jade in, who had promised to turn a blind eye to any illicit monitoring and technical equipment she saw.

As all three watched the CCTV, they immediately recognised Viktor disappearing into the crowd on the busy street. His burly figure, shaven head and sullen expression could not be mistaken. Sue shivered with horror at this brief sight of him.

Nina leant over to the monitor on her desk and studied the images more closely. 'I think I can help with this. I have just got hold of some brand new facial recognition software. It might pick out Viktor from the crowd. If you can get more footage from the direction he was walking.'

After typing on a keyboard, Nina turned to the others. 'I have got several sightings of him. They explain how he might be making a living without being on any official records. They are all around the Gateshead Road area. And guess what? There have been a lot of burglaries there. They have the old MO that Viktor used in Russia.'

'You mean?' asked Jade.

'Cutting the burglar alarm wire no matter how apparently inaccessible, cutting the glass window to put a hand in and release a catch from inside, and stealing mainly small valuable objects.'

'But we have no concrete proof,' said Jade. 'Only Nina's facial recognition technology. It puts him near each of the houses that have recently been burgled. That wouldn't be enough to convict him. We could find him and question him about the attack on Liz, but he might flee the country after an initial police interview. Then we'd lose him forever. The only sure way is to catch him red-handed at the scene of a crime, and remand him in custody.'

'We need to catch him soon,' said Nina. 'Liz is so much better and starting to go out by herself now. I am worried he might come after her and try to finish the job.'

'I've got an idea,' said Sue. 'We know where he's probably doing the burglaries, so why don't we set a trap for him?'

'How?' asked Jade.

'We give him an irresistible place to burgle, and stake it

out.'

'How will we do that?'

'You remember Rula, Countess Malinowska?' Sue asked. 'And that beautiful ornate blue vase she gave me as a present? That's the kind of thing that Viktor would be interested in. Then we borrow an empty house or flat for a week – one that's a very short-term let. Maybe a holiday let. And if we can get hold of it, stick my valuable vase in the window with a camera behind. Then we can watch and see if anybody shows interest. I suspect that Viktor won't be able to resist it.'

'OK. But how do we get the message to him that there's something there – a vase that's worth nicking?' asked Jade.

'I can find people who have holiday flats for rent in that area,' said Nina. 'Sometimes their internet adverts have a poor design. We could offer to upgrade them for free in return for staying there for a week at reduced rate. Then we could re-launch the flat and promote it on relevant websites with some new photos showing Rula's vase in the window. That might get Viktor's attention. Viktor will know the area by now because he has burgled there so much and he would recognise the house in question.'

'I don't know, it's a bit complicated,' said Jade.

'Well, what else have we got?' said Nina. 'As I have said before, in Russia we say that the prey must sometimes become the trapper.'

Sue thought it was worth a try, as she knew that burglars often look online at houses and flats to see if they are empty or easy to break into.

Thus, armed with her camera, Sue took a week off work. She went to the flat in Newcastle which Nina had selected that would benefit from more suitable photos.

The photos showed the interior of a large end terrace. There was some furniture in the house, but Sue added items that would draw the attention of any burglar. These were a range of laptops that Nina had lent her. Jade had told her that these were particularly attractive to criminals as they could be carried away with ease and there was a good market for them.

In the final picture Sue included what she thought to herself was a rather artistic touch. At the side of the house was an oriel window. On the ledge inside, she placed the blue and obviously valuable Russian vase that Rula had given her. She hid a camera in a flower arrangement next to it.

Sue decided to stay in the flat for the rest of the week. She had explained the plan to Liz who would have liked to have joined her, but had to remain in London for continued hospital treatment.

Nina constantly checked images from the camera, and was on a hotline to Sue, who would contact Jade when anyone taking an unusually close interest in the house was detected.

For several nights, Sue saw and heard nothing. She even left the front room light on with the curtains open in the evening, but never saw anything suspicious on the CCTV monitor that she kept at the side of her bed. Nor did Nina, back in London, detect anything on her webcams. Just the occasional curious child or old woman peering in the window, wondering about the vase.

Dejected and tired, on the last night of her stay, Sue told Nina that the whole scheme was a failure and she was going back home tomorrow. Jade had been right. They would have to rethink it all.

She turned off the light, and went to bed. She could not get to sleep, thinking about the failure of the scheme, wasting money on the week's rent, and raising Liz's expectations unnecessarily.

In the darkness, Sue turned to look at the CCTV monitor by her bed. She froze as she saw a dark shape by a bush outside the lounge. She went across to the bedroom window and looked down at the bush. It was probably a shadow cast by the full moon. There had been no shadows at all the last few nights because it had been so cloudy.

Sue gave up on the idea of sleep and went to the kitchen to make herself a milky drink.

She took the drink back to her bedroom and studied the CCTV monitor again. Was it her imagination, or had the shadow changed shape?

As she watched, it moved. It was a man. There was a glint of something in the moonlight. It could be a blade in his hand.

Still clutching her milky drink in one hand, Sue picked

up her phone with the other hand and deftly dialled 999.

'Help me,' she whispered. 'I'm being burgled.'

'Stay calm, madam. Where are you?'

'I'm in my bedroom. I'm alone. There's someone breaking in.'

She gave the police the address.

'We're sending someone now. Keep calm. Can you describe the person you can see?'

'Well, he's bulky, about six feet. I can't see him clearly though.'

'Keep quiet. Don't do anything to alarm him. Keep out of sight.'

'He's after the vase in my window. He's drawn a complete circle in the glass with a cutter of some kind. Now he's got a rubber sucker thing, and he's pulling the glass out so he can get at my vase.'

'Don't do anything to alert him. Keep out of sight. We have people on the way.'

Nevertheless, Sue felt so angry that she didn't heed this advice and crept down the stairs still clutching her milky drink. She opened the lounge door to stare at the window.

She saw a gloved hand holding the sucker trying to lift the cut circle away. But it couldn't because the circle was not yet complete.

Then she saw the figure of a man step forward into the light. Using both hands now, he continued to cut out a full circle. Sue recognised, without a shadow of doubt, the unmistakeable form of Viktor even though he had a beard and was wearing a hat and heavy coat.

The glass circle gave way and his hand was inside the window and on the vase. Sue couldn't help herself. She screamed and threw her hot mug at the hand.

But she missed the vase and the hand. The mug crashed against the window, and smashed the glass.

She heard him shout something in Russian.

As he did so, headlights flared in the street outside and cars screeched to a halt, voices shouting.

'Stop right there! You're under arrest!'

There was a short struggle before Viktor was led away

by two officers and bundled into a police car.

Sue came out of the door to thank the police and gave a statement to a woman police officer.

The next morning, as she travelled back down to London on the train, Jade rang to say that they had found Liz's credit card on Viktor. Evidence that could lead to his conviction.

Some weeks later Viktor appeared in court and pleaded not guilty both to the attack on Liz and to a string of burglaries.

Sue and Nina sat together in the public gallery. Nina had a thick black scarf over part of her face. She had put aside her fear of leaving her flat, determined to see justice done not only for Liz but also for herself.

The two women looked down at Liz who would soon be giving evidence. They saw her face, white as a sheet and her hands trembling. Jade, who was sitting next to her, reached across to hold her hand.

Sue thought back to the conversation she had with Liz several months ago. At that time she had talked about forgiving Viktor, saying some of it had been her fault.

Sue whispered to Nina, 'Let's hope she doesn't back out now.'

They saw Victor smiling and trying to make eye contact with Liz, but she refused to look at him.

She gave detailed evidence of the terrible things that Viktor had done to her in their relationship.

Viktor arrogantly continued to smile at Liz as she continued her harrowing account. However, when he looked up at the public gallery, he recognised Nina. Then his face changed, and he could not hide his shock and fear. Seeing his reaction, Nina felt powerful and vindicated in her tireless pursuit of him. Now she knew that justice would be done. She could leave her voluntary isolation and the darkened room. She would move forward with her life.

Viktor was found guilty, both of the attack on Liz and the burglaries.

When the judge was ready to pass sentence, he asked

Viktor if he had anything to say in his defence.

Viktor said, 'She knows how much I love her. I didn't mean it. I'm a changed man now.'

Liz looked directly at Viktor as the judge passed a lengthy sentence. She met Viktor's gaze with contempt, and laughed at the ultimate lie – that he loved her.

Outside the court in the bright sunshine Sue, Nina and Jade hugged Liz. 'We are so proud of you. You were so strong,' said Sue.

'I couldn't have done it without you,' Liz sobbed.

'We're not just victims of abuse, said Sue. 'We're a team now, and we've won. Now others can have hope!'

ABOUT THE AUTHOR

ROSY STEWART is the collective pen-name of husband-and-wife writing team Rosie Larner and Stuart Larner.

Rosie is a retired social worker and lecturer in Health and Social Care. She worked closely with victims of abuse in Yorkshire, UK. Rosie writes prose, poetry and plays. She was co-leader of a Drama Workshop that welcomed participants of all ages and abilities. She has directed and performed at the Edinburgh Fringe.

Stuart is a chartered psychologist, who worked in the UK Health Service for over thirty years, and was mental health expert in XL for Men magazine. He writes plays ("The Dilemma Advice Show," Beach Hut Theatre 2012, "What Matters is What Floats," Beach Hut Theatre 2013), poems, and stories. His previous book is the cricket novel "Guile and Spin". His most recent book is "The Car: a sonnet sequence with illustrations".

Printed in Great Britain
by Amazon

59528099R00071